SERVE AND PROTECT

BOOK THREE IN THE HEROES OF EVERS,
TEXAS SERIES

LORI RYAN

OTHER BOOKS BY LORI RYAN

The Sutton Billionaires Series:

The Billionaire Deal

Reuniting with the Billionaire

The Billionaire Op

The Billionaire's Rock Star

The Billionaire's Navy SEAL

Falling for the Billionaire's Daughter

The Sutton Capital Intrigue Series:

Cutthroat

Cut and Run

Cut to the Chase

The Sutton Capital on the Line Series:

Pure Vengeance

Latent Danger

The Triple Play Curse Novellas:

Game Changer

Game Maker

Game Clincher

The Heroes of Evers, TX Series:

Love and Protect

Promise and Protect

Honor and Protect (An Evers, TX Novella)

Serve and Protect

Desire and Protect

Cherish and Protect

Treasure and Protect

The Dark Falls, CO Series:

Dark Falls

Dark Burning

Dark Prison

Coming Soon – The Halo Security Series:

Dulce's Defender

Hannah's Hero

Shay's Shelter

Callie's Cover

Grace's Guardian

Sophie's Sentry

Sienna's Sentinal

For the most current list of Lori's books, visit her website: loriryanromance.com.

A NOTE FROM THE AUTHOR

Thank you so much for reading the crazy weird stuff that comes out of my head! It amazes me that you guys keep showing up here book after book to see what my characters are up to, and I truly love you for it! Please keep in touch with me afterward. If you go to my website at loriryanromance.com, you'll see a spot right up front to join my mailing list. I'll send you all kinds of fun stories and updates on my life and the worlds my characters live in. It'll be fun. I promise!

If you love the book, please consider leaving a review at the retailer or website of your choice. It's something that helps authors more than you know!

CHAPTER ONE

Ashley Walker looked out over the surface of the lake to where her siblings floated on inner tubes, a slow smile spreading on her face. She pressed her feet to the sun-warmed wood of the dock and let the heat soak into her skin. The day was perfect.

Well, that wasn't quite true.

Emma was two beats away from pushing Sam to his limit with her nagging, but that was a fairly normal state of affairs. Emma micromanaged. That's who she was. For the most part, all of the Walker siblings tuned her out when she got this way.

"I'm just saying, you could have handled it better." Emma's tone said there wasn't any *"just saying"* about it. She flat-out thought she was right and she planned to make sure Sam knew it.

Sam growled at her. When push came to shove, he'd defend any of them to the end, but Emma walked all over

1

his last nerve, then followed that up with a tap dance. "Carrie Ann knew damned well walking in that I wasn't looking for a relationship. It's not my problem she got buyer's remorse afterward. If she didn't want a one-night stand, she should have walked away the ten or so times I gave her the chance."

"She's your secretary!" The indignation in Emma's voice carried clear across the water. Their other brother, Nathan, was busy working his inner tube behind Sam, whose head lolled back, eyes closed as he appeared to relax in the sun, despite the argument with Emma. No doubt that was egging Emma on even more. She hated nothing more than being ignored.

Sam didn't answer, and Ashley had to agree with Emma a little. Sleeping with his secretary had been a boneheaded move. The woman clearly had *I want marriage and a family* stamped on her forehead, and now Sam had to work with her every day. But men were idiots. That was nothing new.

Ashley watched Nathan paddle, and knew he planned to dunk Sam. Nathan was the youngest of them all at twenty-two, and still the clown of the family. He also couldn't help trying to defuse the argument. But he was underestimating Sam. Ashley knew better. Just because his eyes were closed didn't mean you could take Sam out. You had to wait until that man was dead to the world asleep before trying a stunt like that.

She pressed her lips together, biting them to keep from laughing as she watched Sam's lips twitch the tiniest bit at the edges. Nathan paddled closer, using only the smallest movements of his hands to creep up on Sam. Emma seemed oblivious to Nathan's actions.

Sam turned suddenly and dove onto Nathan's tube, taking them both under the water together, and drenching Emma with the resulting splash. Her sister Cora had been smart enough to paddle slightly upstream to get herself out of the way. Ashley knew she was the smartest of them all for not going into the water with the boys to begin with.

She looked down at her tablet's screen and smiled. In truth, she had other reasons for not joining in the fun today. She had her own party going on online and didn't want to miss a second of it.

The cover of her latest book looked so good, she wanted to cry. Her cover artist had nailed it—from the colors, to the fonts, to the picture of the couple, to the size of her pen name. The bulging biceps of the male model encircled the woman protectively, but she was no mouse. She held a gun comfortably by her side as if it were an extension of her body, perfectly representing the heroine Ashley had penned. She never authored a heroine who was content to simply sit back and let the hero do all the fighting. And in her latest book, the heroine was every bit as well-trained and tough as the hero.

The water splashed when Cora pulled her tube up to the dock, hanging onto the large rope ladder their dad had tied to the wood pylon years before. Cora leaned her head back as she shaded her eyes against the sun.

"How is the release going? Good so far?"

Cora was the only one who knew that Ashley was the

person behind the pen name Leigh Dare. She hadn't really planned to keep the secret from her family and friends for so long. At first, when she'd decided to self-publish romantic suspense novels, she'd been afraid the books wouldn't sell. That she'd be a failure. So it had seemed like a good idea to let that failure be a private thing. And then, when her books had taken off, she'd been so stunned, she hadn't known what to do. Cora, of course, had figured it out. Cora was as avid a reader of romance novels as Ashley was. She'd read the books and spotted several phrases Ashley regularly used, and she'd figured it out by the third book.

Ashley smiled and nodded. "Yeah, people are posting that they love it so far. It's still surreal."

Watching hundreds of people congratulate her on the Leigh Dare Facebook page on her release day was still a dream. It still shocked her that anyone wanted to read her books. The fact that they loved them enough to contact her was unbelievable. Then, as people read the book, they posted their favorite quotes, or came on to tell her they loved it so far.

A few people had begun to tweet the links to their reviews. And those reviews raved about her latest hero and heroine. They loved the way Aiden Kane and Alexa Mayer played off one another. The way the sexual tension built until it exploded as they raced across the country, desperately trying to figure out who was trying to sabotage Dalton Chemical's latest research project.

Cora laughed. "Of course they do. The series is a huge hit, Ash. You're really good. Freakishly good, as a matter of fact," she said, pushing her feet lazily against the dock so that her tube bounced back and forth on the water.

Ashley grinned. "I am, aren't I?" She could say that to her sister because Cora was one of the few people who knew Ashley really wasn't as arrogant as her previous statement made her sound. Cora knew Ashley on a level no one else did. And she knew Ashley was incredibly humbled by her success in this new arena. Humbled and grateful beyond words, so she chose to go the tactless joke route instead.

Ashley's phone rang and she glanced at the screen before putting it back down. When Cora gave her that raised brow look that said *fess up*, Ashley rolled her eyes. They'd always had a weird ability to communicate, even though they weren't related by blood. When Ashley had first come to the Walkers as a foster child, she'd hated Cora. Resented her. In fact, at one time or another, all of the Walker children had been so at odds, no one would have thought they'd ever be as happy as they were now.

Within the first year, Cora had knocked down Ash's defenses. They were as different as night and day, both physically and in personality, but their bond was strong.

"It's Alice," she mumbled. Mumbling was not at all like Ashley. She spoke loud and clear and put out whatever she was feeling or thinking for the world's consumption. Without hesitation. Without censorship. But the recent calls from her former social worker, Alice Johnson—three of them in just as many days—made her want to close in on herself.

Cora's forehead wrinkled up. "Ah. I get it," she said after a moment. "It's almost your anniversary."

Ashley pressed her lips together and nodded. "I just don't want to revisit it this year, you know? She hasn't called the past few years, so I'm not entirely sure that's why she's calling now, but I just, well, you know."

Cora did know. None of the Walker kids wanted to be reminded of the reasons they had become Walkers in the first place. Their pasts weren't fun, by any means. But they were all happy to be Walkers now. Theirs was a family truly built on love. Blood, sweat, tears, and love. They celebrated that, having moved past their backgrounds, for the most part. But sometimes their former social workers thought about them around their "anniversary dates" and got in touch. Ashley was fairly sure they didn't even do it consciously. They wouldn't ever seek to hurt the kids they'd helped. But as much as they were all grateful to the people who had helped them get out of the situations they'd been in, they weren't eager to revisit those times.

"Maybe she's figured out your secret and wants to congratulate the next *New York Times* bestselling author," Cora said with a grin.

Ashley laughed, with a glance to her siblings to be sure they were far enough away they didn't overhear Cora. "Yeah, maybe you're right. It's probably not related to my anniversary date at all. I'll call her," she said, dismissing the alert on her phone that told her she had a new voicemail. "But not until we get back. I just want to relax for now."

Now it was Cora's turn to laugh. "You mean watch your

book's rank obsessively, read every blog post or review posted, and stalk your favorite readers online to see if they mention *Dead Run* in any comments or posts?"

Ashley grinned. "Exactly. Relax."

She grabbed the reading glasses that sat near her Kindle —this pair hot pink with white temples—and shoved her feet back into her flip-flops. She stood and shaded her eyes, looking down at Cora, who still bobbed on the gentle waters of the lake. Emma and Sam still fought in the background, and she could hear Nathan joking around, trying to distract the pair.

"It's my turn to cook," she said as she looked toward the lake house that was her family's vacation home. It was only twenty minutes away from their home in Evers, Texas, and it was more a rustic cabin than lake house, with a kitchen, open common room, and two bedrooms, but it was all theirs. Their parents had the master bedroom and all five kids still bunked in the other bedroom, drawing straws over the two sets of bunk beds and one full bed that took up the entire floor space of the room. It wasn't anything to brag about, but it was a treasured family haven.

Cora wrinkled her nose. "Foil meals or baked spaghetti?"

"Foil meals," Ashley answered with a grin. She was the only one in her family who still stuck to the two meals she'd learned how to make as a teen. Everyone else had managed to add to their repertoire, but she loved the comfort of the meals her mom had taught her to make. They were camping staples, and to her, camping staples were what their time at the lake house called for.

Cora laughed and shoved off from the dock to rejoin the rest of their family floating several yards away. Ashley waved to the group and then headed up to the kitchen to start cooking. With any luck, her mom would be there and they could chat while Ashley got dinner going. Besides, her mom made a much better salad than Ashley did. Her siblings would be happier with dinner if her mom had a hand in it.

GARRET HENSLEY WALKED into the station house and tossed his gym bag onto the warped surface of his desk. The place didn't exactly scream *modern*, and lately, he'd felt a bit like his body was going the way of the station house. He kept in shape, so it wasn't so much that as it was the lack of stimulation. The lack of anything other than work in his life. It wasn't like he got out much or socialized with anyone who didn't wear a badge or work in a crime lab. People who didn't know the smell of a dead body or what it was like to chase down a junkie intent on slipping from your grasp.

That hadn't bothered him much in the past, but lately, he'd begun to notice. Hensley had been one of six detective sergeants in the Branson Falls Criminal Investigations Division for five years. He loved the work, but his life was stagnant—empty, somehow. And for some unknown reason, he felt a hell of a lot older than his thirty-three years.

He ran a hand down his face and looked around the bullpen at the desks of the other detectives and the two animal services officers who also shared the space. They all had the look of people who'd been overworked and underpaid for far too long. Of men and women who'd spent a few too many hours inside. Well, that wasn't entirely true. The animal services officers had tans.

At least he had kept his physique, Garret thought as he eyed the guts forming on the frames of two of the men taking up space at the desks across from him. He hit the gym or ran every morning without fail. He wouldn't give in to the temptation to place his sleep over his physical fitness. Not when he'd had to give up healthy eating due to the demands of a job that had him dining from a takeout bag at the drive-through more often than not. The least he could do each day was run the calories off, even when the job kept his sleeping hours to a minimum.

There was a needling thought at the back of his mind that his life needed to change, but he pushed it aside. He'd been doing this a long time. It was what he knew. The detectives of the CID covered crimes, from robbery, assault, up to homicide for Branson Falls and the surrounding towns for miles. They often had to drive an hour or more to investigate crimes on limited resources and a shoestring budget. It wasn't a job someone did for money or luxuries.

In fact, Garret wasn't entirely sure why he did the job anymore. But that thought would have to wait. His captain stood in the doorway to his office, and barked, "Hensley!" His standard call to action when they'd caught a case.

Garret's partner, Doug Mann, wasn't in the bullpen yet. He'd get the info from the captain, then rustle up Doug and head out. Knowing Doug, the older man was probably in the can with his morning paper. Doug was pretty committed to his morning ritual. Another thing Garret was purposefully ignoring was Doug's upcoming retirement. In six months he'd be breaking in a new partner and saying goodbye to the man who'd had his back in more ways than he could count for years.

Captain Sharp had lowered his six-foot-four frame into the creaking wooden chair behind the government-issue metal desk that took up most of his office. He didn't look up as he rattled off Garret's assignment.

"One-eight-seven at the apartments over on Guadalupe." *Homicide.*

Garret was glad Sharp hadn't looked up. He didn't catch the way Garret's body swayed at his words. A homicide at the apartment building where Garret grew up. The building where Alice Johnson—a woman who was more mother to him than his own had ever been—lived. He put a hand on the back of the chair in front of the desk and gripped it. Hard.

He hadn't known his father—other than to know the Irish spelling of Garret's name had come courtesy of his father's Irish roots, which as an adult had struck him as odd, since his mother had given him her British last name. He'd buried his mother when he was nineteen, and other than a few aunts and uncles he never saw, Alice was the only thing resembling family he had left in this world.

"Got a number?" *Please not 207. Please God.* Even to know she was close to violence like that would be too much. But if it were her... No, *that* he couldn't handle.

His Captain read from the notepad by his phone. "Two—"

God, please, no. Please. His hands gripped, squeezing the crap out of the back of the chair in an effort to—well, he didn't know what. To ward off the blow? How could he possibly do that? There was no way to ward off what was coming.

"Oh-seven."

CHAPTER TWO

Evie jumped as her mother slammed the door behind her.

"Don't you put that there, Evie. I told you, you keep your things in your room. Bill doesn't want to look at your pictures."

Evie nodded at her mom and took the picture she'd drawn in school that day off the refrigerator. She looked at the colors she'd chosen again before folding it up and tucking it into her backpack. The cabin she and her mom had stayed in wasn't purple, but she'd drawn it that way anyway. Purple was better than brown. And she'd put bright pink flowers around the outside of the cabin, even though those didn't really exist either. Her version had a roof, too. One without holes.

"Sit down at the table and eat your sandwich, then get on up to your room. I don't need you messing this up for me again."

Evie sat in her chair at the kitchen table and swung her legs back and forth. She picked at the corner of the sandwich. Peanut butter.

Her mom kept talking as she fussed at some papers on the kitchen table, shoving them into a folder like the ones Evie's teacher used at school. Maybe her mother was going to be a teacher. She'd never seen her with a folder like that before. That would be exciting. Her mother had worked jobs here and there, but never something as fun as being a teacher.

"You stay up in that room tonight, girl. I'm cooking special for Bill tonight. Real special. You keep out of sight."

Evie nodded. The smell of something good cooking made her stomach rumble, but she didn't think her mother was going to give her any of it. She cooked for Bill, but that's because her mom wanted that ring on her finger. Evie didn't really know what that meant. If she wanted a ring so bad, maybe she should just go out and get a ring. But her mother seemed to want Bill's ring. That ring must be special.

At the sound of a car in the driveway, Evie grabbed her sandwich and her backpack and left the room before her mother could chase her out. She went to her bedroom and shut the door, but the thin wood wasn't enough to keep the voices out. Bill was loud when he talked.

"What the fuck is this shit? Am I made of fucking money?"

"No, baby. It wasn't expensive, I promise. There was a sale on the steaks and I used coupons. You sit, baby, and I'll get your plate ready." Her mother was using that weird, wispy voice she used when she talked to a man.

Evie put her sandwich on her nightstand and dug out the apple she'd gotten at school today. Her teacher brought Evie two pieces of fruit every day. One to eat at lunch and one for dinner.

A plate clattered on the table downstairs, as though dropped instead of placed. Evie cover her ears against the sound of Bill's taunting words as plates clattered and her mother's wispy words floated out of the kitchen. The scrape of a chair.

"Get under the table, and make it up to me." Bill laughed and Evie wondered what was under the table that could help her mother make anything up to Bill. And why was that funny to him?

She tried not to listen, although she didn't really know why. There was always something in Bill's voice that scared Evie. She never minded that her mother didn't want her near him. She wished they could go back to it just being the two of them. Her mother wasn't any nicer when they were living in the old car they'd once had, or staying out at the cabin, but at least it was just the two of them. She didn't have to wonder if Bill would come home and throw things and yell.

Her mother's voice was muffled now but she still crooned in that weird voice. Then there was a bump as though something was hitting the underside of the table and Bill's laughter came up the stairs. Evie took her apple and her sandwich and crawled into the closet, shutting the door. It was dark in there and that wasn't fun, but it blocked the sound better. She almost couldn't hear his laughter in here. It wasn't happy laughter, somehow. It was mean. Evie didn't understand it. Why laugh if you're not happy?

"Thank you, Haddie! Try to behave yourself over there," Ashley called across the main room of the Evers Public Library. As the librarian, one would think she would encourage quiet whispers rather than friendly hollers across the room, but that hadn't ever been her style. Her library was a place for people to gather and chat, visit, and even— gasp—*hum* as they perused the shelves for a new read. If they wanted quiet, they could use the reading room in the back.

She'd even instituted a monthly teen dance party in the library, despite the objections of the more traditional town leaders. On the third Friday of every month, the lights were dimmed over the stacks, the music came on, and the town's teens could dance and party in a safe environment. When she was able to show that library usage had increased as a result, everyone in town had not only been on board, some even tried to claim credit for the idea. Ashley didn't much care who took credit. She just wanted people to feel welcome. To see the library as the sanctuary she always felt it was.

Growing up, no matter what foster home she was in,

Ashley had always been able to find solace in the town library. She'd learned early on that she just needed proof of residency and she could get a card. And getting that card meant losing herself in a world of fantasy and make-believe. A world where anything was possible. A world where none of the realities of her life could touch her.

Hadeline Gertrude Gillman, otherwise known as Haddie, waved a hand in reply and gave a little "whoop-whoop" as she went out the front door with Sheriff John Davies on her arm. The action drew a laugh and headshake from Ashley. She wasn't entirely sure of Haddie's age, but the white hair with a pink tinge to it and the frail frame hinted at eighty-something. After volunteering in the library each morning, she would head on over to the senior center for a few hours. Today it was John's turn to escort the older woman. Tomorrow, Lily Winn, the town's new veterinarian, would walk Haddie over.

Ashley glanced around the main room. A few patrons had their heads in newspapers or books, but no one looked like they'd need her anytime soon. The Evers Bees—a group of women who sewed handmade quilts out of upcycled fabrics they then donated to families in need—were in the side room working away on their latest project. And another volunteer was shelving books on the far wall.

Ashley stepped into her office behind the circulation desk and shut the door. She'd be able to see anyone approach through the glass pane in the top half of the door, but for now, her priority was reaching Alice. She'd felt guilty as soon as she'd listened to Alice's voicemail two days before. She should have listened to her messages before coming home from her weekend at the lake house. But she hadn't. She'd put Alice off and now felt awful.

The woman's last message had sounded...well...*off*. All she'd said was that she needed Ashley to return her call, please, but there was something underlying her tone. Something in her voice that told Ashley there was more to this call than just hello or how are you.

She hit Alice's contact on her cell phone and listened to the phone ring once again. For two days she'd tried to reach her, but Alice wasn't answering her calls and she hadn't returned them either. Could she be sick? Ashley suddenly had an image of Alice hurt and needing help. She wasn't a frail woman, by any means, but she did live on her own and she wasn't exactly young. She wasn't old either, though. If she had fallen or hurt herself in some way, would she have been able to get to the phone to call for help?

Ashley shook her head, trying to shake off the feeling of unease that swept over her. No. Alice was in good health the last time Ashley had seen her. That had been—oh, wow —that had been close to a year ago, she realized. She frowned and looked at the clock. In three hours, her part-time employee would be in and there would be two additional volunteers on site. That was the soonest she could slip away.

She put her phone in her back pocket—something she normally didn't do while at work—and stepped back out to the circulation desk. She would make the drive to Branson Falls this afternoon, just to be on the safe side. If nothing else, she could take Alice out to dinner. They were long overdue for a visit anyway. And at least she could put her mind at ease and be sure her old caseworker was all right. Make sure it was just her insane workload that was keeping her from returning Ashley's calls.

CHAPTER THREE

G arret ground out his question through a jaw much too tight with the tension of this case. With the grief that was burying his heart.

"You can't remember anything else about the car?" Because *it was small* didn't really help a whole hell of a lot, and Garret had nothing to go on so far.

His partner looked on as the loser in front of them shrugged. Again. The man made Garret think of a squirrel, for some reason. Maybe it was the slightly bucked teeth or the somewhat fuzzy brown hair that seemed like a tail as it poofed out behind the man in a loose braid. *What man braids his hair?*

His partner returned the look. Doug had known right away who Alice was and why Garret had no business whatsoever being part of her murder investigation, much less heading it up. Luckily for Garret, they'd been partners a long time. Doug knew there was no way in hell anyone would be able to drag Garret off this case. So he had kept his mouth shut with the captain, and here they were, trying to find out who would stab a woman like Alice Johnson to death. A woman who'd never done anything but give of herself to those around her. A woman who hadn't deserved the brutal end she'd met three days before.

And they had squat to go on. Alice appeared to have let her assailant in her home. There was no evidence anyone had tampered with the locks or forced their way in. In fact, the person seemed to have caught Alice off guard with the attack, because there was little evidence of a struggle. The teapot sat by the stove, filled with water. Two mugs stood ready with bags, waiting for her to pour the brew. She had been stabbed fourteen times with one of her own knives from the large wooden knife block that Garret had looked at over the years during meals in Alice's home.

The cuts had begun tentatively, but by the third slice, they showed evidence of a killer who had let loose and wasn't showing restraint any longer. Defensive wounds had been limited to a gash on her right arm and a few cuts on her left hand, as though Alice had been slow to defend herself. As if shock or disbelief had delayed her reaction.

Contrary to popular belief, thanks to crime shows on television, an assailant didn't always leave fingerprints on any surface they touched. If the environmental conditions weren't right, prints wouldn't appear. If the assailant didn't touch something just right, a print wasn't going to show up clearly enough to run a match. And this person had had the wherewithal to wash the knife—handle, blade, and all—in Alice's sink before leaving.

Garret was hopeful the crime scene guys might turn up a bit of blood or skin cells in crevices of the handle that hadn't been washed away, but that would take weeks. Months, maybe. Another common misconception perpetuated by cop shows was the twenty-four- to forty-eight-hour turnaround from the lab. That was a joke.

"Can you remember anything else that seemed out of place that day?" Doug asked the squirrel. They had asked this guy the question in various forms several times already. In fact, this was their second time canvasing the neighbors, so they'd interviewed him before. But the key to solving cases often lay in interviews. Mind-numbingly boring interviews. You asked the same questions over and over. Open-ended questions, targeted questions, follow-up questions. You asked if there's anyone else you should talk to. And you chased the leads. Followed them wherever they go. Because fingerprints and DNA analysis, as sexy as they were, took a long, long time. And most of the time, they weren't going to be there.

The guy never got a chance to answer the question, because the interview was interrupted by banging. Loud banging on his apartment door.

"Hello! Please, is anyone home?"

The distress in the woman's voice was clear. Garret's hand went to his sidearm as Doug moved the squirrel away from the door and asked if he was expecting anyone.

"Please!" More banging.

Garret moved next to the door and opened it. A striking woman—all long, black hair and glass-blue eyes—all but tumbled into the apartment. He scanned the hallway behind her as his arm shot out to catch hold of her. Nothing there. Nothing but the crime scene tape and evidence seal on the door of Alice's apartment across the hall.

He looked down at the fragile woman in his arms. No, that wasn't right. She looked fragile at first glance, but she wasn't. She shoved back and held herself stiffly in front of him, eying him and Doug with the suspicion worn only by someone who'd dealt with the system. And then her face seemed to crumple as though she'd made some connection she hadn't wanted to. She shook her head at him, as if by denying what she was seeing, she could make it go away.

"Where is Alice?" Her voice trembled with the question.

He shouldn't give out any information. But her wariness told him she'd been one of Alice's kids. And her current appearance—put together, well dressed, successful—told him Alice had gotten this one out. Out of what, he didn't know, but it was clear at some point, this woman had gotten things together.

He was drawn to her, felt horrible for what he knew she would need to learn. Because something told him the information about Alice's death would hit her as hard as it had hit him. He was inclined to be gentler with her than he might have been with someone else, and it ate at him. Why would he want to be gentle with this woman he didn't even know? A woman who might very well have information that could help him solve this case?

"What's your name, ma'am?" he asked, but she stepped away from him, one arm wrapping around her stomach, and he could see tears welling, ready to spill over. She backed toward the door and stood next to it as if she might flee. He allowed her the position. For now.

"What happened to Alice?" she asked again, as she wilted in front of his eyes.

He looked over at Doug, knowing they shouldn't give out that information just yet. But both wanting to know who she was and whether she might be able to help them with their case.

"She got stabbed," called out the not-very-helpful, likely stoned squirrel-man next to Doug. Garret would have rolled his eyes if he'd had time. But he didn't. He needed to grab hold of the Snow White look-alike in front of him as her knees seemed to buckle. She clung to his arm, her eyes wildly swiveling from his face to Doug's. Now the tears did fall, as she looked for them to deny what the squirrel had said. *Shit.*

Neither one of them was in a position to confirm or deny anything just yet. She was a completely unknown person walking into the middle of an ongoing and open investigation. He brought her over to the squirrel's couch and lowered her onto the cushions. Kneeling before her, he placed a hand on her leg, mostly to draw her attention to him. To ground her as she continued to look like a trapped animal ready to strike out for her own safety.

"Stabbed in her own kitchen, dude," called the squirrel, as if trying to help. "We don't even know if any of us are safe here." He was not helping.

He heard the woman begin to whisper *no*, over and over.

"Doug, you wanna do something about that?" Garret called out over his shoulder, not taking his eyes off Snow White. He heard Doug guide squirrel-man into his kitchen, where he knew his partner would keep him busy and see if he could get any more information out of him.

He needed to get her name, but she was white as a sheet and her hands covered her mouth as she continued to whisper her chant of *no*. He was back to thinking she looked like a china doll who might break if handled the wrong way. Demanding to see identification probably wasn't going to get him results. He'd need to take another tack if he wanted to find out anything from her.

"My name is Detective Garret Hensley, ma'am. Are you a friend of Ms. Johnson's?"

And bam. The transformation from Snow White to Ice Queen was instantaneous and palpable. She turned cold, crystalline eyes on him. The eyes of someone who'd learned as a kid you don't talk to cops. Yeah, she was one of Alice's kids. He'd bet a few paychecks on that.

"Do you have any suspects in custody?"

Interesting way to ask the question. Not *do you know who killed her?* or *who did this?* No. She wanted to know if they had any suspects in custody. He was sure she wasn't law enforcement. She didn't carry herself the right way.

Didn't cover her six like a LEO would. But she wasn't simply a citizen, either.

He answered her question with a question. "When was the last time you saw Ms. Johnson?"

Referring to Alice as *Ms. Johnson* gutted him. She wasn't just a victim he was trying to find justice for. This was *Alice.* He didn't know if it was the effect Snow White was having on him, or the fact that he was investigating Alice's death, but he was off-balance. Way off-balance.

Snow White seemed to be assessing him, so he held still and let her look, then watched as she seemed to make a decision.

"I haven't seen her in almost a year." She offered no further information. Simply answered the question he'd asked. She used two fingers from each hand to swipe at the tears under her eyes and pulled herself together. He had a feeling she wouldn't let him see her cry again. As though she'd remembered where she was, and her barriers were now in place.

"Have you talked to her in that time, Ms.—" He drew out the last, essentially asking her name once again.

She looked at him and ignored the question as to her identity. "She left me a voicemail the other day. A few, actually. But she didn't answer when I tried to call her back." She tried to hide her feelings. He could see it in the hard set of her face. But the anguish in her eyes and the way her voice cracked belied her cool veneer.

He took out his pad and jotted down a note. "Can you tell me what day she left that message?"

He moved to sit beside her on the couch and held his pen ready to write as much as she'd give him. As many details as he could get from her. If Alice was trying to reach this woman, maybe she was connected to what had happened in some way.

"She left me a few messages over the weekend. Two on Friday and one on Sunday."

"Did she say what she was calling about?"

She shook her head no. "She just asked me to call her."

"Was that unusual? You said you hadn't seen her in a year. Did you speak frequently?"

Snow White pressed her lips together and shook her head. She was an intriguing combination of stone walls and helpless dismay, of steely nerves and vulnerability.

"No, it wasn't unusual. It was that time of year."

"I don't know what that means, Ms.—" He needed to get her name before she left, and he would prefer not to have to pull the *I need to see identification* line.

She relented. "Walker. Ashley Walker."

"Ashley Walker. What do you mean, that time of year?"

"You know that Alice was a social worker?" She paused while he nodded. "Well, social workers seem to think about their kids on big anniversaries, whether they realize they're doing it or not. At least, Alice always did. For me, it was the anniversary of my adoption by the Walkers. Alice tended to call then, just to check in."

"And it's close to your, uh, anniversary?"

She nodded her head. "Yes, it was last week."

She didn't offer any other information, but she did have questions of her own.

"Do you have any leads? Anything to go on?"

"I'm afraid I can't answer that question, Ms. Walker." *As much as I want to.* He had no idea what her draw was. Why he wanted to tell her everything they knew. Hell, he wanted to unload and let her know all of his frustrations with the case. To let her know he was struggling to handle his feelings, to balance the need to remain professional with the need to bring the scumbag who had taken his friend from him to justice.

"So that's a no?"

"It's an *I can't answer the question*," he said, giving her his most apologetic smile. The one that oozed charm and usually had women falling at his feet. She didn't fall. She narrowed her eyes at him with a look that told him she had opinions about cops and they weren't good.

He convinced her to give him her contact information for follow up, should he need it, but her demeanor remained cool.

"Is there anyone you'd like me to call for you, Ms. Walker? Do you need help getting home?" He was an idiot. He was asking because he wanted to know if she had a husband or boyfriend. Where the hell had that come from?

She shook her head.

Doug came out of the kitchen and stood quietly, waiting for Garret to signal they were finished. He stood and offered Ashley Walker his business card.

"Please contact me if you think of anything else," he

said, giving her the standard line as he walked her out of the squirrel's apartment with Doug at his back. Her eyes fell to the door opposite them and she swallowed visibly. He watched her beat back tears, then kept his eyes on her as she walked away from him, her arms wrapped tightly around herself, head high.

ASHLEY HADN'T BEEN able to drive home from Alice's apartment building. She drove around the corner before pulling over and breaking down. Then she'd called Cora and tried to explain through choked sobs where she was. After ten minutes, she'd gotten it out, and Cora and Nathan had driven the hour and a half to pick her up and drive her car home for her.

What she was feeling was a combination of grief, guilt for not answering Alice's calls, and horror at the fact that Alice had been so brutally murdered. But most of all, she was beginning to feel rage. Rage and anger that someone could take the life of a woman who was so good to so many people. Without Alice's unconditional love and support, Ashley would be dead. She was sure of it. She would have killed herself if Alice hadn't gotten her out of the situation she was in years before. Whether it was by burying herself in pills or a bottle, or achieved more directly, it would have happened. Alice had given her the chance at a life of love and security. A chance to be safe. It was something Ashley had known she'd never be able to repay.

But Alice never asked for anything in return. It was simply what she did. And standing by the gravesite two days later, watching as mourner after mourner walked up and placed a rose on her casket, Ashley knew Alice would be smiling down on them all. She would smile to see so many of her former kids here. Because Ashley had no doubt that's what many of the people in attendance were. When you came from that world, you could spot its inhabitants, even after you'd gotten out. There were people ranging in age from their teens to their late sixties. The older ones would be coworkers. But many of the younger people were the kids. Alice's kids.

Ashley looked around at the group and saw people from all walks of life. Artists, rebels, nerds, and jocks. People who clearly hadn't fully escaped the life Alice had hoped they would. And those who looked like they'd somehow found their way. Some held small babies in their arms, and Ashley could imagine Alice's response to them. She'd reach for all of them, to rub their tiny heads or run the back of a finger down a soft cheek.

This was Alice's legacy, Ashley thought. This was what she'd worked for. They were here for her.

She felt him watching her long before she saw him. Garret Hensley, with his dark hair cut short and tight, clean-shaven face, and dark gray eyes. He looked like he needed about three days of sleep, and she wondered if he had anything to go on in Alice's murder investigation. Probably not, she thought. If he was here, looking so haggard and worn, then he was looking for a thread to pull. He was hoping for a break.

She looked at the crowd as people began to work their way back to their cars and wondered if the person who took Alice's life was here. A shudder tore through her and she felt her father's arm around her. She tilted her head and let it fall to his shoulder. She'd been one of Alice's luckiest kids. Not everyone landed in a family like the Walkers. Most didn't. Her father squeezed her shoulders and she looked up at him.

"Ready to go home, kiddo?"

Her nose burned and her eyes filled once again with tears at the question. All of Frank Walker's children were his "kiddos", no matter their age. And she'd never been as happy for that as she was today. She wasn't alone, and that felt really good. Her mother came up alongside them as they turned toward the two cars the family had piled into for the ride here. Her siblings already waited by them. They'd all come, even though Alice hadn't been a part of their lives, for the most part.

"Ashley!"

She didn't need to turn around to know who was calling her. Her father's arm tightened protectively, but she reassured him as she watched Detective Hensley walk toward her. His pace was brisk, like he thought she might turn and run any minute, and he wanted to be sure she didn't get away.

"I'll meet you over by the cars, Mom and Dad. That's

the detective working on Alice's case. I want to see if he has any updates."

Her mother and father exchanged a glance but Ashley squeezed her mother's hand. "I'll be fine. I'll be just a minute."

They turned and left just as the detective caught up to her. She brushed her hair out of her eyes and tipped her head back to look up at him. The man wasn't overly tall, but compared to her short frame, his five-foot-ten height caused her to look up. He was sturdily built and looked like he could take on a tank and come out the winner.

"Ashley, I'm glad I caught you." He looked past her to where her parents and siblings were waiting, and his eyes held an unasked question. Ashley waved at them before turning back to Garret.

"My family," she said, the words reminding her that Alice had given her that. The greatest gift imaginable. One she'd grown up thinking she would never have. That had been all Alice's doing.

He nodded. "I just wanted to see if you remembered anything else. Anything that might help."

"Then, you have nothing so far?" she asked.

"Nothing solid yet. A witness said they saw a small car parked in the lot that isn't normally there. Could be something. Could be nothing. And *small car* isn't going to get us anywhere. We're still waiting on a few other things, but so far, there's not much to go on."

She nodded and looked past the detective to where his

partner waited for him. Dave, she thought. Or Doug, maybe? She wasn't sure. Now Garret Hensley, she remembered. And that bothered her. A lot. She shouldn't be so focused on this man. He should be nothing more than the detective investigating Alice's case to her. And yet, she found herself looking into his eyes and thinking they looked kinder than she'd expected for a battered cop. And she wondered what had left the scar that cut a thin, white line through his upper lip. She wondered a whole lot of things she had no business wondering.

"I should go," she said suddenly. "I need to go."

He nodded, but his eyes assessed her and she felt uncomfortable in her skin. It wasn't a feeling she was used to. Not as an adult. Not as Ashley Walker. As Ashley O'Rourke, she'd felt it often. But never as Ashley Walker. She felt as though he suspected her of something, though she couldn't say why.

"Just let me know," he said, "if you think of anything."

She nodded as she backed away, aware of his eyes on her. Aware of an intensity in his gaze that made her uneasy. Did he look at everyone like that, or just her? Ashley turned and walked into the embrace of her siblings and parents and had to fight the urge to turn back to see if Garret was still watching her. She needn't have worried, of course. As soon as they were piled into the back of her parents' car, Cora turned to her.

"Who is that man and why is he still watching you?"

Leave it to Cora to ask.

CHAPTER FOUR

A shley took a deep breath and sat back as Cora drove them toward Pies and Pints a week after the funeral. She needed this. A night out with friends. She hadn't felt like herself since she'd found out about Alice and she hated that. She wanted to feel normal again. On the other hand, she felt guilty for wanting to feel normal when Alice wouldn't feel anything ever again.

Ugh. She shook off the feelings and slid her flip-flops off her feet, drawing one foot up under her. Today should be a happy day.

"So," Cora began, chewing on her bottom lip. A sure sign she had a confession to make.

Ashley raised her brows and looked at Cora. "Soooo?" she said, drawing out the single syllable and making it a question.

"Soooo," Cora said again, drawing it out herself this time.

"Alright, chickadee, cut to the chase. What are you hiding?"

Cora attempted an affronted tone. "What? Nothing." She actually had the nerve to go for a *why would you think I was up to anything? That's pure silliness* look and Ashley just stared back blandly at her. Cora was utterly unable to lie. She simply didn't have the lying gene in her DNA.

"Oh, fine. I just think it's time for you to tell everyone about your books. You just made the *USA Today* bestseller list, for heaven's sake. Why are you hiding something like that?"

"Cora?"

"Yes?"

"You already told them, didn't you?"

"Well, it's not my fault."

Ashley grinned, unable to find it in her to be upset. "How is it not your fault?"

"Because it's your fault, really. I mean, who keeps it a secret that they're publishing a book? No, not *a* book. *Many* books. Many highly successful and now *USA Today* winning books."

"It's not *winning*," Ashley said, shaking her head. "It's *bestselling*."

"Winning, bestselling, same thing. The point is, there might be cake."

"Cake?" Again with the eyebrows going up. "There might be cake."

"Okay, will be. There will be cake."

And there was. A cake in the shape of a book. And all of

Ashley's family and friends were at Pies and Pints to cele-
brate. Ashley grinned as she took in their congratulations.
Cora had long since given up trying to defend herself for
leaking the information. She was now simply saying it was a
sister's prerogative to out an author, and she didn't know
what the fuss was about.

Ashley was okay with it. Screw it. Who cared if Haddie,
her mother, and many of the women her mother went to
church with had read her books. Sex scenes and all. And the
sex scenes were...well, they weren't mild. They weren't *Fifty
Shades* and all that, but they were steamy. There was a hint
of kink here and there. But whatever. She had never been
one to shy away from attention, and she didn't filter herself
in person, so why would she ever think of filtering her voice
as a writer?

She did squirm a little when Haddie sniffed and said
she'd read worse. Ashley didn't want to think about Haddie
reading her sex scenes or any others.

Good grief. And when her mother whispered that she
might read a few of the scenes to her father, Ashley covered
her ears and threatened to annul the adoption, or whatever
process one would seek when their adoptive parents
became too horrifyingly embarrassing. What a shame to
have to undo the adoption now after all this time.

She did get a few good laughs out of the evening,
though. Her brothers wanted to know who had taught her
"those things" and they weren't the least bit amused when
Ashley insisted they'd have to be more specific than "those
things" if they wanted answers. Emma began to recount all

of the ex-boyfriends Ashley had had in high school and hypothesized about which ones might have taught her which things. Cora found all of that hysterical and couldn't stop laughing, especially when Ashley began to nod her head yes, or shake her head no vigorously at one name or another.

She mentioned she might set up some readings at the library, making it a Couples' Night Out kind of thing. That had gotten her father and brothers to spit beer and sputter, as her mother and sisters laughed harder. John Davies shook his head and grinned at Ashley before grabbing his wife, Katelyn, and saying something about writing their own love scenes at home.

CHAPTER FIVE

Ashley looked at the squat, red-brick building and suppressed the memories that tried to flood her. She hadn't been in this building in years. Not since the day she'd finally come to Alice and accepted help. And that was a day she didn't want to relive for anything. But she would.

Because Alice deserved more than to be found lying dead on her floor with no one to pay for taking her life. Ashley sucked in a deep breath and pulled open the glass door with the worn letters indicating that the offices beyond were those of DFPS: Texas Department of Family and Protective Services.

She moved silently down the hall, looking for the face of the woman she'd met a few times with Alice.

Marlis. The woman's name was Marlis, which Ashley had always found different, but sort of hypnotizing. She just hoped Marlis still worked here and that she might have some idea of what was going on with Alice's case.

There. Red hair and a wild skirt and blouse. That's what Ashley remembered about Marlis. Wild in every way.

"Excuse me?"

"Yeah, child?"

Ashley smiled. That was the other thing Ashley always remembered about Marlis. She was paler than a ghost, with obvious Irish roots, but her manner of speaking didn't match those roots at all.

"Marlis? My name is—"

"Ashley Walker!" the woman exclaimed before Ashley could tell her who she was. "Of course I know who you are, child. Of course. You one of Alice's special'uns."

Ashley smiled, a little taken aback.

"And that new book! Steamy and hot, that Aiden of yours."

"What?" Ashley had to fight the urge to step back. "Alice knew I was writing?"

Marlis laughed. "Of course she did, child. Alice knew everything. She always watched over her kids, even after they's on their way in the world."

Maybe Alice had been calling her that weekend to congratulate her on her book release, just like Cora had said. It seemed more people had figured out her secret than Ashley realized. She smiled to herself, happy that Alice had known about her books. It seemed important somehow.

"I just wanted to see if you knew if they'd found out anything more about Alice's murder," Ashley said, forcing herself not to flinch at the word. "Do you have any idea what she was working on? Any ideas the police might not have looked into?"

"Taking over my job, Ashley?"

Ashley jumped and spun to face Garret Hensley. Good grief, was the man everywhere? She ignored the fact that his button-down shirt stretched across his chest and biceps in a way that made her want to unbutton it pretty damned quick. She'd have to remember that look for a future book.

Then it dawned on her. Alice had been killed two weeks ago. Why was he only coming to her office now?

"Are you serious?" She practically sputtered the question.

He tilted his head, cocking a brow at her. "Excuse me?"

"You're just coming to interview her coworkers now? Are you kidding me? The chances that Alice's death are related to something with her job are something like—" Wow, she sucked at math. "—well, really, really high. And you're just now coming to talk to the people she works with?"

Garret gave her that carefully bland look she was sure he practiced at home in front of the mirror, but she doubted he was happy with the criticism. What man ever was? She squirmed. *Damn it.*

"Well?" she said, hands on hips and foot tapping because it was all she could think to do. When in doubt, dig a deeper hole. "Don't you know that most police work relies on interviewing people? Over and over. You interview anyone and everyone you can because DNA and fingerprints probably aren't going to get you a suspect for a while, if ever. You've got to do the leg work."

Garret again wondered why this woman seemed to know so much about police procedures as he tamped down the frustration that came with being told how to do his job. It was par for the course. No one ever thought cops were doing enough.

She intrigued him, though. She spoke with apparent knowledge on the subject, but she wasn't a cop. That much was clear. Even if he hadn't run a background check on her, he would know that. She didn't have the stance or demeanor of someone who walked the thin blue line. Maybe she had friends on the force?

As he studied her, Marlis handed him a stack of files. "I managed to narrow things down a bit for you, Garret. There were several files that were inactive on her desk, and a few that are just minor follow-ups. These are the cases that might cause the kind of hard feelings you asked about."

He reached around Ashley, leaning in and allowing his arm to graze hers as he took the files from Marlis. His eyes stayed glued to Ashley, an open challenge in them now.

"You mean the cases I asked about the last time I was here, interviewing everyone? My *third* visit since Alice died?"

Ashley's gasp was audible and her eyes went wide, but Garret wasn't entirely sure her response was solely due to his words. If she was feeling half the heat arcing between their bodies that he was, her gasp could easily be a response to that. Or maybe she was feeling the same urge to rock her hips into his and press their bodies together. To see if he could find an ounce of relief from this insane drive to plunge into her. *Holy hell.*

He stepped back, holding the file folders in front of him, praying it looked casual. If Ashley and Maris and the half-dozen other people around him caught on to the fact that he was hiding the hard-on of all hard-ons behind those folders, they didn't let on. Thank God.

"Since you seem to understand a great deal about the investigative process," he said, narrowing his eyes on the woman before him, "I'm sure you also realize these things take time. It's not a TV show where everything is wrapped up in forty-five minutes. You want to tell me why it is you seem to know so much about how a murder investigation works, Ashley?"

Marlis answered for her.

"Because she's a bestselling author! She writes the most amazing romantic mystery stuff."

"Stuff?" Garret repeated, and let out a bark of laughter. "Since when do authors get things right? They glorify everything for the sake of sales, not accuracy."

Ah, there she was again. The Ice Queen. No, wait, she looked more like fire than ice right now. Hands back to hips, an inch or so added to her diminutive frame, and that spark in her eyes.

"Romantic suspense. I write romantic suspense. And I put a lot of time and effort into getting the details right. I check and double-check and talk to officers who know what they're doing. They help me get the details right. For my last book, I had to talk to a detective, an explosives expert, a psychologist, a lawyer, a medical examiner, and an arson investigator. I don't just write fluffy nonsense with facts I pull out of the air. I research."

"Huh. Anything I might have read?"

She let her gaze run up and down his body, pausing noticeably on the part still covered by the file folders. From the look she affected, she found him wanting. But he didn't buy it. Her breathing had shallowed slightly and the tiny lick of her lips hadn't been intentional. She couldn't hide her attraction to him.

"I don't know. Do you read steamy romance novels? You know, bodice rippers?"

She said bodice rippers as though some might consider them a bad thing. Hell, he didn't know what a bodice ripper was, but it sounded pretty good to him. Especially if the steamy parts were coming from her mind. He wanted in that mind. Now.

He took a step back. He needed to get out of here and regroup. Big time. This woman did strange things to him and he wasn't entirely comfortable with the notion. She didn't just draw him in sexually, the way most beautiful women did. She drew him mind, body, and soul. On a level and with an intensity that was unsettling.

"No. I guess not," she said with a Cheshire Cat grin. And suddenly, she'd turned the tables on him. She held that grin as she swept around him, called a goodbye to Marlis, and walked away. Again.

It seemed to him he was frequently watching her walk away.

CHAPTER SIX

Ashley waved to the volunteer taking over for her while she went on her lunch break and scooted out the door before someone grabbed her. People had a tendency to latch on and want to talk for hours at a time right when she was set to leave the library. Especially since the news of her alter ego as Leigh Dare had come out. Everyone had a story idea they wanted to talk to her about, or a book they wanted her to co-write with them. Extricating herself was proving more and more difficult. Not that Ashley was known for her tact.

She'd begun to simply smile and say something vague along the lines of, "okay, bye!" before hauling butt away from people. That was rude, even by her standards. She'd heard whispers that she was spending too much time with Haddie—someone well known for having no internal filter and no tact. Ashley was choosing to take it as a compliment since Haddie was one of her favorite people.

She switched out her glasses—purple with white polka dots today—for a pair of white-and-black paisley sunglasses, and pushed through the front door of the library. The portulaca planted by the town's volunteer greens committee was in full bloom, splashing bright orange, pink, and yellow splotches of color throughout the garden beds in front of the library.

It was quiet outside for a Tuesday afternoon, but she guessed everyone was already inside the diner or hiding from the heat in the barbeque place down the street. She walked the half block to the crosswalk and then across the street toward where she was meeting her friends, Laura and Katelyn, for lunch. She vaguely wondered if the monthly art walk hosted by the town's galleries and artists was this coming Friday or the following one. She'd need to remember to ask Katelyn if she needed help with refreshments.

As she reached out her hand to the diner door, Ashley paused and looked around. Nothing. But every sense in her body had suddenly gone on high alert. She looked back in the direction she'd come and held herself still, searching for some small sign of...of, well, she didn't know what. But, *something*. There was something there. She was sure of it. The feeling of being watched had taken hold of her, and wouldn't let go.

"Ashley?"

Ashley screamed as she swung toward the voice. Her heart slammed into her rib cage and she put one hand out toward Garret and one hand to her chest as she tried to steady herself.

His arms came up immediately and his face showed nothing but concern.

"Ashley, are you okay? What's wrong?" He scooped her to his chest protectively as he covered her with his body, and looked where she'd been looking only seconds before.

She pushed herself out of his arms and looked back at the library. "It's nothing. I think I freaked myself out, but it was nothing."

He looked down at her pale face and trembling hands and knew it wasn't nothing. She was well and truly spooked.

"What are you doing here?" she asked, looking at him as though he might be some kind of criminal instead of the officer of the law she knew him to be. It was a fair question. Evers was a good hour and a half drive from Branson Falls.

"I had to come out on a burglary call about halfway between Branson Falls and here, so I just kept on driving afterward. Thought I'd come check out Evers. Maybe check out its library," he said with a grin.

And its librarian.

The color was returning to her face and as Garret looked around he saw no sign of anything out of the ordinary. Maybe she had gotten herself worked up over nothing.

"Hey, Ashley, everything all right?" A blonde woman and a brunette came out of the diner door and looked back and forth between him and Ashley.

"Yeah, guys, I'm sorry. I was on my way in and ran into Mike Hammer, here."

Smiles appeared as the women looked at him.

"Really, Ashley? Mike Hammer?" He grinned at her and stuck his hand out to one of the women. "Detective Garret Hensley." He didn't know why he added the detective part. He didn't normally feel the need to slap a title on himself when he wasn't on the job, but something about Ashley always made him feel like he was scrambling sideways off a cliff.

The blonde woman shot a look at Ashley while she shook his hand.

"Reeeeeally?" Blondie drew that word out a little longer than strictly necessary. "Detective Garret Hensley. Ashley hasn't told us a thing about you."

Now why did that feel like a kick to the gut? What was he, in high school?

The brunette took his hand next. "I would have thought Ashley would mention meeting a sexy detective. Ashley, you want to fill us in here?"

Ashley laughed and shook her head. "No. I don't. You can stop whatever you're thinking. Detective Hensley is working on Alice's case. He was just in the area and stopped by to say hello. And now, he's leaving."

The other women seemed to sober at the mention of Alice and introduced themselves as Laura Bishop and Katelyn Davies.

"Are you John Davies's wife, by any chance?" Garret asked the brunette.

The woman smiled. "Yes. You know John?"

"I knew you looked familiar. He and I met a couple months back at a state-run crisis and negotiations workshop. He showed everyone there your picture and talked about you any chance he got."

All three women laughed at that.

"They're newlyweds," Ashley said.

"Nah," said Garret shaking his head. "It wasn't the newlywed thing. He's head over heels. That guy'll be bragging on you long after the honeymoon is over." He winked at Katelyn, who blushed, then turned to Ashley. "I have to get going. Are you sure you're all right?" He did one more scan of the street behind them as he spoke, but she nodded.

"I'm fine. Working on too many suspense plots in my head, is all. I just need to remember I'm supposed to scare my readers, not me."

He nodded. Then his mouth kept talking, despite the fact that he was pretty sure his brain hadn't sent any instructions to it. "Do you want to go to dinner with me Saturday night?"

Shoot, maybe his mouth was onto something here. Maybe he'd just shut his brain off and let his body run with this.

Or not. If the look of shock on Ashley's face meant anything, his mouth needed to shut up and let his brain resume control.

Before she could answer, Laura answered for her. "Oh, she'd love to."

"I would?" Ashley looked as dumbstruck as he felt, but

51

Garret was just gonna run with this. He had an opening and he'd take it.

"Great," he said, backing away before she could object. "I'll pick you up at seven at your place."

"But, I...wait. What?"

"She'll see you then! You have the address?" Katelyn asked, apparently on board with Laura's plan, whatever that plan was.

"Got it," he said, since he had her address from the background check he'd run on her, and turned to jog away. That was probably the dumbest thing he'd done in a long time, but screw it. She wasn't a suspect in the case. She'd been checked out and cleared early on. Nothing was stopping him from taking her out. And the damn woman hadn't left his thoughts since he'd first seen those bewitching blue eyes of hers. Screw it.

Ashley rounded on her friends, hands on hips. Again. She seemed to be using that position a lot lately.

"What in the world do you think you're doing?"

Neither answered.

"Are those new sunglasses?" Laura tried. "I just love those. Where did you find them?"

"Not going to work, Laura. What were you thinking? I can't go out with him," Ashley hissed as Katelyn ducked her head and studied her shoes.

"Of course you can. He's gorgeous and sweet and intelligent and—"

"You got all of that from two minutes and a *hello, how do you do?*"

"How do you do?" Katelyn asked with a snicker.

Laura kept right on going trying to distract Ashley.

"Oh, is that Presley Royale over there? Should we invite her to lunch?"

Damn. She'd hit Ashley's weak spot. Defending Presley Royale when everyone else around town thought she was a wealthy snob was something Ashley took seriously. Ashley had long ago figured out that Presley was uncomfortable around other people, but not in a snobbish way. She was shy. As simple as that. The woman who everyone had assumed had everything she needed, everything anyone could want, needed the one thing her father couldn't buy her. True friends. Ashley couldn't ignore Presley, and Laura knew it. With a sigh, she turned and called across the street, letting the matter of her "date" with Garret drop for now.

"Hey, Pres, what are you doing in town?"

The tall woman brightened and looked both ways before crossing the street to them. There was a light about her face that Ashley hadn't seen before.

"Hello, Ashley, Laura, Katelyn." She nodded to each of them in turn and Ashley knew why people thought she was a snob. She was stiff and polite, with a formality to her interactions that Ashley suspected came from her upbringing. Her father owned Royale Stables and Presley was his prized champion right alongside his horses. She was a many-times national champion in the show ring, and the pride of her father's stables. It disgusted Ashley how little Presley's father valued his daughter as a person. He valued only what her reputation brought to his business, but not the person beneath.

"We're grabbing lunch. Wanna join us?"

Presley shook her head, but she was smiling. "I'm meeting Lily Winn for lunch, but thank you for the invitation."

"How did you pry Lily away from Carter's side for lunch?" Katelyn asked with a laugh. When Lily moved to town to take over the local veterinary practice, she and Deputy Carter Jenkins had begun dating. They'd been pretty inseparable since then. The thought brought a smile to Ashley's face. The couple reminded her of the love she wrote about in her books, and she was hoping they'd hear news about a happily ever after for them soon.

"I begged, if you must know," Presley said. "I wanted to pick her brain about writing a business plan."

"Do tell." Katelyn said exactly what Ashley had been thinking. "You're thinking of opening a business?"

Presley looked distinctly uncomfortable in the hot seat, and Ashley let her off the hook. "You'll tell us about it when you're ready, won't you?"

"Absolutely," Presley said, the breath she let out letting Ash know she was grateful for the save.

"Ok, but lunch another time. We need to catch up."

"I'd love that," Presley said, and they all said their goodbyes.

As the group walked into the diner, Ashley realized Laura's goal had been accomplished. The topic of her coerced date with Garret had been dropped. *Darn.*

CHAPTER SEVEN

She really should have cancelled this. Ashley tugged at the straps of her sundress, then whisked it off, tossing it onto the pile of discarded clothes on her bed. She was ridiculously nervous about this non-date, as she'd started to think of it. It couldn't be a date if she hadn't said yes in the first place. So it was a non-date. Just two friendly people going out for a friendly meal. As friends. Most definitely not as lovers. Not even remotely.

Then why was she on her sixth outfit? She surveyed the wreckage of her attempts to look sexy and attractive, but in a totally one-hundred-percent casual, I-just-want-to-be-friends sort of way. That's what she was going for. The jeans and black blouse had looked too casual. The white flouncy skirt paired with the coral sweater had looked too dressy. Leggings with a tunic sweater looked perfect, but were much too hot for the middle of the summer. She growled in frustration and pulled the sundress back on, then slammed her feet into a pair of flip-flops.

"Good enough."

This date—no, *non-date*—was causing her too much stress. And she knew why, too, but she wouldn't admit it to herself. Admitting that she was entirely too damned attracted to Garret Hensley would put her in an even worse mood. Admitting that she was feeling sick to her stomach in anticipation of this date—worse still. When he had wrapped his arms around her protectively the other day, she had gone from the creepy feeling that she was being watched to tingling for a whole other reason entirely. From his hard body pressed to hers. From the protective alpha streak she saw oozing from him. That streak she wrote about in her books. Damn, it was as powerful as she'd made it out to be.

So why was she so spooked by that? *Well, gee, Ashley, could it be because you haven't ever been that attracted to a man?* She snorted.

"Yeah, that's an understatement of epic proportions."

Not that attracted? Try never even *remotely* tingly. She'd had a lot of sex as a teen. She cringed to admit it to herself. Too much. Her poor parents had been dealing with the backlash and rebellion that came from what she'd been through in foster care. And it had taken a long time for her to realize she needed to stop. That intimacy with a man wouldn't come from baring her body to him and letting him stick his penis in her. That true intimacy was so much more than sexual acts.

By the time she'd gone off to college, she had begun to

get it. She needed to value herself, value her body and her mind, before being with a man. She needed to find intimacy and closeness first, without the sex part getting in the way.

The problem with Garret Hensley? He made her want to tear her clothes off. And his clothes, too. Because one look at him and she knew there was something magnificent hiding underneath that fabric. He was all hard lines and muscled chest, and she'd be willing to bet her paycheck that he was sporting a damned fine six-pack under those clothes.

That brought her thoughts to that sexy vee of muscles that pointed like an arrow down to a man's... *Oh for the love of—*

The doorbell interrupted her thoughts and she had to swallow hard to get her bearings. Man, she needed to stop thinking about Garret without his clothes. About that hard flesh. Would it be warm and hot and smooth when she ran her hands over it? Of course it would. Or maybe he'd have a smattering of hair on his chest. He seemed like a smattering of hair kind of guy...

Oh heck. This was not good. The doorbell rang again and Ashley grabbed her purse and held it in front of her, hugging it tightly to her body to try to ward off the effects of Garret Hensley.

Damn Laura.

"Hi," she said as she swung the door wide.

Oh.

My.

Toes.

The man stood in dark blue jeans and a cream-colored

button-down shirt that hugged his chest. Great. Another reminder of what lay beneath. Good heavens, she needed to be less dramatic. But really. Did the man need to show up looking like that? The shirt had the look of one that had been worn many times, and her fingers itched to reach out and slide her hands over it. Just to see if it felt as soft and worn as it looked. Sure. It was the fabric she wanted to check.

Good grief, Ashley.

"Hi."

Ohhhhh. This is bad.

Somehow, his voice had dropped an octave since she'd last heard it. It was now a *come hither* voice. It was a *trust me, you want to lie back and open your legs for me* voice.

Bad legs. Very, very bad legs. She pressed her legs together and chastised them to no avail.

There was a distinct hint of laughter in his eyes as he watched her, then cracked a grin her way. Maybe it was the fact that she had yet to say a word to the man. "Ready?"

For what?

"Um, yeah. All ready." *Sigh.* She might as well just admit defeat right now, and concede she'd be up for anything with this man. *Ready for anything.*

Scenes from her books whipped though her mind as they walked to his car. Heaven help her, he put his hand on her back as he reached to open the passenger door for her. And of course, he let that hand run up and down her back once, virtually freezing her on the spot. Only, there wasn't any freezing going on. There was heat. Sizzling heat branding her back and racing straight through her body, settling—well, *damn*. Settling right smack between her legs.

He looked at her quizzically now. "You sure you're all set, Ashley?"

"Oh yeah. I'm good." She sat in the car and pulled the edge of her sundress in as he shut the door and rounded the car to join her.

"So," Garret said as he drove them to the restaurant. "Why a librarian?"

"I like the whole sexy librarian fantasy thing. You know. The bun done up tight, eyeglasses, then whip the hair down while Van Halen's *Hot for Teacher* plays in the background."

The car swerved a little and Ashley laughed.

"Not nice, Ashley. Not nice."

The moment helped cut the tension. She allowed herself a few more laughs at his expense as he scowled at her, then gave him the actual answer.

"I just always loved the library growing up. It was a place I could escape to, no matter what was going on in my life."

He squirmed in his seat and she wondered what was making him so uncomfortable.

"Problem?"

"I, uh, I should probably tell you, I had to run a background check on you for the case."

Ashley nodded slowly, not at all sure how she felt about that.

He went on as she tried to gauge her feelings. Exactly

how much did he know about her? As if reading her mind, he rushed to assure her.

"I don't know a lot of details. Just employment stuff and education, and, uh, that you were in the foster care system. That you were adopted. I didn't look further than that, Ashley. I swear. Just far enough to know that you were who you said you were, and what your connection to Alice was. Just enough to see if you had a criminal record, to clear you as a suspect."

Ashley blew out a breath. She appreciated his up-front manner, and she would have told him the same information tonight if he'd asked, so she supposed it didn't matter. She'd always been open with people about her background and her adoption. It was the details of how she came to the Walkers that she never shared with anyone. In fact, even Alice hadn't known the full story. But Ashley was one-hundred-percent sure Garret was telling the truth. If he knew the full story, there was no way he'd be able to look her in the eye. No way he'd be able to hide the horror and the disgust.

She nodded again, this time faster. Probably a little too fast.

"Okay."

"Are you sure?" he asked as he parked the car outside a small restaurant she'd been to a handful of times. It was two towns over from Evers, and she remembered the food being excellent both times she'd come. He turned in his seat after putting the car in park and looked at her.

"I'm sure," she said, brushing off the haze of memories

that clung to her. She wasn't going to revisit those ghosts. Not here. Not now. They were ghosts best left in the dark. She opened her door and smiled. "Let's eat. I'm famished."

GARRET FELT a little like a man set out to sea clinging to nothing more than an inflatable rubber ducky and one of those stupid pool noodles to paddle with. He was taking on water and going down. Fast.

Ashley made his head spin. In a good way. She was sexy and funny and irreverent. So damned irreverent.

Not to mention, he could look at her all damned day and then some. Her eyes always grabbed him, but as they talked at dinner, he realized how full her lips were. Whenever she quirked a smile at him, he found himself watching the way her lips stretched wide and he had to stifle the urge to lean over and kiss them. That would be where he'd start. He'd kiss the corner, then slide his tongue along the seam, seeking—no, begging—entrance.

"So, are you going to become my police procedural expert for all my future books?" Ashley asked him as she closed her menu and set it aside.

Oh, he'd like to be an expert for her books, but it wasn't police procedure he wanted to consult on. He'd ended up downloading one of her books to his eReader. He usually read thrillers and mysteries, but he'd been missing out. Her books had the mystery and suspense elements he liked, but they were sexy as hell, too. He wouldn't mind helping her test future scenes before her books came out.

He mentally smacked the crap out of himself and refocused on Ashley. "Of course. But from what I've seen, you have your facts right, so you must have a good resource already."

He watched as she froze, her water glass midway to her lips. Then a slow flush crawled up her cheeks, lighting her up with a warm glow as her eyes flew to his over the rim of her glass.

"You read my books?"

"Not all of them." He grinned. "I've read *Dead On* and *Dead Heat* so far. I'm just starting on *Dead Target*. So, let's see. That leaves *Dead on Arrival* and *Dead Run,* right?"

She looked at him with wide eyes and repeated herself. "You read my books?" There was a slight squeak to her tone that made him laugh.

"Yes. I read them and I liked them. They're damn good. And really freaking hot."

She squeaked again. No words this time. Just a squeak.

Garret laughed and looked up as the waitress came to take their order. When she walked away, he leaned back in his seat and picked up the topic of her books, but from a different angle. "So do they always have a happy ending? The guy gets the girl and all that?"

"All that?" She grinned. "Yes. They always have a happy ending. The guy gets the girl and they live happily ever after. It's a nice fantasy, don't you think?"

"Is that all it is? A fantasy?"

There was something in her eyes when she answered. It flashed there, dark and ugly for a split second before it vanished. "Some people get lucky, I guess. My parents are definitely in love. They've got their happily ever after."

He nodded. He didn't need to ask, but he did. "But you don't think you'll get yours, do you?"

Her fingers fidgeted with her glass, but she seemed to catch herself and dropped her hands to her lap. He half thought if he looked under the table, he would see her clenching them together.

She didn't answer him, but let the question hang out there, substituting one of her own instead. "So, if romance novels aren't your usual fare, what do you normally read?"

He accepted the shift and answered with his own smile. "Most of the time I'm reading forensics reports, but when I can read, I like action-adventure, thrillers, mysteries—that kind of thing."

They continued to chat over their meal, and he walked her to her front step at the end of the night, waiting to hear the click of her lock before going back to his car. But he couldn't help but return to that moment in the conversation when she'd shifted topics. Because he was sure the unspoken answer to his question was no, she didn't see a happily ever after in her own cards. And for reasons he couldn't articulate and didn't really want to speculate on, that made him sad. Incredibly, troublingly sad.

CHAPTER EIGHT

"What the fuck is this? What the hell did you do to yourself?" Bill's words were slurred and ugly, making Evie glad she was already in her room for the night. She agreed with him. Her mom looked funny. Not like herself at all. She'd snapped at Evie when she asked her about it.

Evie dragged her backpack into the closet and shut the door. The voices became more muffled as she tried to ignore her mom's explanation for her new hair color. It was black. Completely black. And she was wearing glasses. Evie had often asked her mom if she could have a pair of glasses. Missy Tobin, a girl from her old school, had worn glasses and Evie thought they looked neat. Like having bionic eyes. She would get blue or purple glasses if she ever got them.

Her mom's were plain black and really thick. They looked funny.

She unzipped her backpack and put her headphones

over her ears. She didn't have anything to plug them into, so there was no music or anything, but they muffled the sounds coming from the living room a bit more. Her mother's words weren't quite so loud with the headphones on, even though her mom was laughing with that fake laugh she used only with Bill. Evie knew that soon, the moaning and groans would come from Bill, followed by more of that high-pitched baby talk her mom thought men liked.

And maybe they did like it. Her mom was pretty good at getting men. But she didn't keep them for very long. They'd been with Bill for a while, though. Months now, she thought, although she didn't really know for sure. But it had been cold when they'd stayed in the cabin, and it was warm out now, so that must mean months had passed.

Maybe if Bill didn't like her mom's new glasses, she'd give them to Evie and she could wear them to school and be as popular as Missy Tobin. Maybe then she'd look smart and the kids wouldn't make fun of her so much.

Mrs. Walters had given her a banana that day. She pulled it out and started to eat. A loud thud on the stairs followed by giggling told her Bill and her mom were coming upstairs. She hoped Bill passed out soon. She wanted to sneak downstairs and get something more to eat. Her mom had been too busy with the hair dye in the bathroom to make her much dinner. She'd only had some potato chips. If she could sneak downstairs after they went to bed she could make a bowl of cereal or a sandwich.

Whoomp, whoomp, whoomp. The rhythmic thunking of the bed told her they'd made it into his room. She finished her banana and drew her knees up to her chest, then wrapped her arms around her head, pressing the head-phones more tightly to her ears with her elbows. The noise almost disappeared completely when she did that. Just a few more minutes, she hoped. Just another few minutes.

ASHLEY DIDN'T HAVE flashbacks very often, but with Alice's death, she seemed to be a little stuck in the past and overly sensitive to a lot of things. The clatter of a spoon hitting the floor as she and Cora set the table for dinner at their mom's house had been enough to send her hurtling into the past. Her stomach bottomed out and nausea hit instantly. The slap across her face for dropping the silver-ware seemed so real to her. As though her foster mother had only just hit her that moment, not years—more than a decade now—in the past.

Then her mother's hands were brushing her arms, massaging softly as she whispered to her. Her words brought Ashley back to the present. Cora had left the room. They all liked privacy when they were having these moments, and even though they were now adults, the holdover from when they were young still stuck. If they were in the room when one of them had a flashback or a meltdown, they would either help if they were the only person there, or bug out if they weren't.

"All better, sweetheart?" her mom asked lightly.

Ashley felt her chin start to tremble as she sank into a

chair. "I can't believe that just happened. It's been so long," she whispered. Then anger and frustration hit. "It's been so long!"

This time, the heat of her anger filled her words and she no longer whispered. Her mother pulled a chair close and sat with her, taking her hands into her own.

"Alice's death is bound to have raised some issues."

"But I'm not a child anymore, Mom. I should be able to handle this. I should be able to turn it off."

Her mom shook her head. "Maybe that's the problem, Ash. Maybe instead of trying to shut it off, you need to face what you're feeling. Alice's death stirred things up. And that's okay."

Now it was Ashley shaking her head. "I faced it all back then. I don't want to go back. I don't want to think about it or face it again. I'm done with that."

Her mother looked at her quietly for a long time before speaking. "Did you, Ashley? I know you went to your counselor, and I saw improvement back then, so I didn't push. But I've always felt like there was something you weren't fully processing. Like there was something you didn't want to deal with."

Ashley didn't respond.

"Alice mentioned it to me once, as well. When she took you out of that last house, she knew there was something you weren't saying. She told me she never pressed because she had the grounds to remove you, and she revoked their foster license, but she knew something happened that you didn't tell her about."

Ashley felt her whole body go numb. It was a feeling she was familiar with, only she'd just about managed to forget it. She knew on some level that her mother deserved a response. After all she'd been through with Ashley, heaven knew she deserved better than this, but Ashley was in shut-down mode. She went blank. Blank eyes. Blank mind. Blank heart. She was gone.

CHAPTER NINE

Ashley was drained by the time she got home hours later. She'd ruined dinner with her family. Even though her mom had given her time to come back out of her cocoon, it hadn't been the same and they both knew it. Ashley went through the motions of the meal and managed a few bites, but the tension was palpable. No one had asked her about it, but Cora had given her a longer-than-usual hug before she left, and Ashley had had to fight tears at several points.

She wasn't used to this. She'd been out of that world—a world that required her to close herself off from others—for so long. The thought that Alice's death had dredged all of that up terrified Ashley. She didn't want to be that person anymore. But in truth, she wasn't sure she knew how to avoid it.

She pulled her car into the driveway of her small house and turned off the engine. She needed to find a way to snap herself out of this funk, she thought as she walked up the front steps. She stopped suddenly when she realized there was something lying on the welcome mat outside her door.

Oh God. Was it a kitten? Whatever it was, it wasn't moving. She'd forgotten to turn the outside light on before leaving the house this afternoon, so she fished her cell phone out and woke it with a swipe of the screen. She tilted the light toward the lump on her mat and jumped back when she saw what it was.

Revulsion swept through her and she spun, looking for any sign of who might have put it there. Because that rat hadn't cut its own head off and fallen on her doorstep. That much was certain. She could hear her breath coming in audible pants as she scanned the street. She hadn't seen any other cars as she pulled up, but she searched for any signs of life now.

Nothing. The block was quiet. She couldn't tell if the hairs on the back of her neck were standing on end because someone was actually watching her, or because she'd gotten herself worked up.

She turned back to the rat and swallowed her disgust at the sight of it. She was torn between disgust and pity for the poor thing. It had died a horrible death. Who would do something like that? She put her key in her lock and stepped over the rat, into the house. It took her only moments to grab some gloves and a garbage bag from under the sink. When she tossed the body into the garbage can at the side of the house, she threw the rubber kitchen gloves in, too. She wouldn't be using those again.

The outdoor light she'd flicked on illuminated the whole driveway. She still saw nothing. No cars that shouldn't be there. Nobody lingering on the sidewalk or hidden in the bushes. No sign that anyone had been here at all. She only wished she could try to convince herself she'd imagined it, but there was nothing imaginary about a decapitated rat.

After scrubbing her hands with hot soapy water, she sat in front of her computer and fired it up. She could probably be distracted by a little time on Facebook. One thing Ashley had discovered since becoming an author: she was never alone. She never needed to feel alone again. If her family or friends weren't around, she had friends across the country she could touch base with. Some were other authors. Some were readers who had become fans, and eventually, true friends. And the funny thing was, they were all different ages, from all walks of life.

The first friend she ran across when she logged on was a fellow romance author who had reached out to Ashley when she was a brand-new author in the romance writers' realm. Ruth was online and had posted a clip of her daughter stomping on a sand castle they had just built. Her little girl was now five and as precocious as Ruth herself. The little girl laughed and said she was getting rid of her Italian villa because she wanted to build herself a leaning tower of pizza for lunch.

Ashley laughed and typed *add some gelato turrets and a chocolate fudge moat for dessert, beautiful girl* in the comments section. Then she clicked over to the newsfeed and followed it down, scrolling past negative posts and looking for pretty pictures and fun videos. Before long, she'd found an adorable meme of a ferret looking affronted and saying, "I said good day, sir!" and another of a dog splayed out on the floor with a line that read, "Please don't make me adult today."

Within an hour, she'd forgotten about the rat prank. She wasn't completely over that wrung-out feeling she'd had since talking to her mom, but she was laughing as she went to get ready for bed.

ASHLEY'S RELIEF lasted through her morning routine of coffee, shower, more coffee, clothes, makeup, and more coffee. Things came crashing to a disastrous halt when she opened her front door to find the rat was back on the steps, with the plastic bag she'd tossed it in torn open to expose the dead body.

Ashley's head shot up to look at the street, but that bravery lasted only a minute before she slammed the door and locked herself in the house. Because if that rat was back, that meant someone had fished it out of her trash last night. And that likely meant they'd watched her throw it in the trash and then come and taken it out while she was inside.

She tried to shake off the feeling of having her privacy— her space and sanctuary—invaded, but the feeling hung thick in the air. She didn't often have trouble with anyone, but occasionally, a teenager decided to smoke a cigarette in the library bathroom, or do things they had no business doing locked in a storage closet with another teenager. Ashley rarely felt the need to call parents, but every once in a while, she did. She would bet this was one of those teens getting back at her. That didn't make it any less frightening.

She looked at her phone and thought about calling John Davies. Her mind flitted to Garret instead, and it wasn't simply because he was also a police officer. She was thinking that having his arms around her would be a comfort. And that feeling kind of freaked her out. Heck, there was no *kind of* about it. She was freaked out on so many levels right now, she didn't want to think about any of it.

She shoved her phone and lunch into her big tote bag and opened the door slowly, taking another look around the yard and driveway. Nothing in sight. Ashley locked the door in a hurry and picked up the edges of the bag with the rat in it. Holding it away from her body, she placed it in the garbage can and then hopped in the car. She normally walked to work when the weather was nice, but for right now, the idea of being out in the open and exposed frightened her.

Fear, and a residual feeling of edginess, stayed with her throughout much of the morning. It was summertime, so she didn't get the usual afternoon influx of teenagers coming in to do homework and projects for school. She did, however, have a group of teens that came in for a bit while waiting for one of the local cycling groups to start. They filled water bottles from the water fountain in the lobby and waved hello to her before heading back out to start their trip. Ashley waved and smiled back at them, but hated that she also found herself eyeing each one of them, trying to assess their potential for hacking off the head of a rat and tormenting her with it.

She didn't want to be questioning the feelings of every teen that walked in the door. It just felt awful. Ashley prided herself on making the library a welcoming spot in town. It wasn't your traditional silent space where she shushed patrons over a pair of glasses perched at the tip of her nose. Sure, she wore glasses, but they were fun and funky frames she changed regularly. And she never shushed. She ran a shush-free library and liked it that way.

But for the life of her, she couldn't figure out why anyone other than a disgruntled teen would leave a carcass on her steps.

"Are you okay?" Ashley jumped at the question, then turned to face Haddie, who had been volunteering in the reading room with a group of elementary-aged kids.

"Oh, Haddie," she said, one hand on her heart. "For the love of Pete, woman, don't scare me like that."

Haddie tossed her pink-tinged cloud of hair as though she had gorgeous locks cascading down her back instead of a large poof that only moved a smidge before bouncing back into place. "Would you look at me? Do I look like I'm sneaking up on anyone with a cane that lets everyone know I'm coming and the damn creaking in my hips that I swear sounds like that woman in that movie? What's that one? In the church?"

Ashley was never sure how, but for some reason she could always guess the movie references Haddie was making with the scattered tidbits the older woman remembered. "*Sixteen Candles*," she said, referring to the scene where Molly Ringwald goes back into the church for her sister's veil and runs into that little lady from *Poltergeist* whose shoes squeak as she walks.

"Exactly. So don't you *woman* me. Why are you so quiet today? Something's off."

Ashley smiled. She and Haddie spent a lot of time together. She'd bonded with her early on after starting work at the library. Haddie had even less of an internal filter than Ashley. When Ashley was the person trying to do the filtering in a relationship, well, that was extreme to say the least. It certainly wasn't something to be proud of. And yet, Haddie could care less. She loved her irreverence and if she was honest, Ashley loved it, too.

"I'm fine, Haddie." She laughed, feeling lighter than she had all day. She certainly wasn't going to tell Haddie about the dead rat and get her all freaked out, too. She was overreacting. Letting herself worry all day like this had been foolish. She walked with Haddie out to the front steps and waved as her friend left with one of the other volunteers on her arm. The afternoon sun was still shining, so she spent a few minutes deadheading the flowers out front before going back inside. The library would be empty for much of the rest of the afternoon. She was caught up on her work, so she planned to spend the next few hours perched at the circulation desk, laptop in front of her, as she brainstormed her next plot. She was thinking she might need a female cop as her next heroine. Or maybe a female FBI agent. No, ATF. A woman who knew her way around a weapon or two would be cool.

By the time she looked up from her computer, it was ten minutes before closing time. Only one or two patrons had interrupted her and she'd taken the vague idea of a female ATF agent and matched her up with a hero strong enough to match her heroine's personality. She had a rough sketch of a plot that included the sabotage of the nation's water ports and railway system by a zealot hell-bent on interrupting US trade abroad to support his isolationist beliefs. It was still a work in progress with a great many holes. By the end, the plot would most likely look nothing like it did now. But her creative juices were flowing, and that's all she needed at this stage of the game. With time, her characters —even the bad guy—would start to speak to her, and she'd develop things further.

Ashley saved her work and shut down her computer, waving goodbye as the last of the patrons left through the front doors. She needed to walk the building and make sure no one was left in the stacks or in any of the meeting rooms or the children's area. The quiet never unsettled her at the end of the night. Her library had always been a sanctuary for her.

But on this night, as she began working her way through the building, shutting off one light after the other, she felt trepidation creep up her spine and wheedle its way into her brain. She wondered if it wouldn't be a bad idea to leave a few of the lights on in the library overnight. Then again, if she did, chances were John Davies or one of his deputies would come through thinking that something was wrong.

She forced herself to flip off the light in the children's area, realizing she could hear her own breaths. She was breathing heavily and her heart was galloping at a much faster pace than it usually did. She laughed at herself, trying to break the anxious edge the air had taken on. Only it felt more like she was choking than laughing. She moved as quickly as she could into the main room, rounding the corner planning to douse the lights and grab her things before locking up for the night.

She didn't scream when she hit the body. Her sharp intake of air was the only sound she made before she struck out. She'd learned a lot of things as a foster kid.

One habit that she'd started young and had held on to— she didn't make a sound. She never screamed or cried out. She wasn't sure what had started it, exactly. She supposed she'd simply learned at some point that it didn't help. Not in the world she'd lived in as a child. A lot of the time, it only made things worse. If her attacker got off on pain, on fear... then showing it in any way only egged the person on.

No, she had learned long ago to clamp down on the fear and the pain and fight. Fight hard. And don't stop fighting until you're the only one standing.

She lashed out now, not having used these skills for so many years. Too many years. Her hits were weak. Certainly nowhere near strong enough to take on her attacker. He was tall, stronger than a teenager. His body was thick and built, not the lean body of an adolescent. She'd been wrong. Whoever was messing with her head hadn't been a teenager after all. Whoever this was, she was pitifully outclassed in weight and strength. She wouldn't be winning this fight.

CHAPTER TEN

A shley's fist hit Garret solidly under the chin and he stepped back, hands raised. The library had been empty when he'd arrived, so he had begun to walk toward the back rooms in search of Ashley. Before he could even call out to her, she'd plowed around the corner and come out swinging hard. At him.

As his teeth clashed together under the surprising blow, his body wanted to fall into the familiar patterns that would deflect and return the assault, but he forced himself to hold his arms at bay.

"Ashley!"

She didn't stop. She raised one leg and spun, and he recognized the move. His arms came down to deflect the blow. If her foot had connected with his knee at that angle, he would have been in a world of pain.

"Ashley!" He shouted now, needing to cut through whatever was going on in her head. Her eyes were wild as she struck out at him, but she seemed to startle at his shout and step back.

"Ashley," he said now, quietly. The emotions on her face wavered from one extreme to the next. Fear, then shock, and briefly mortification. But mortification was left in the wake, as anger took hold and remained.

"What the heck, Garret? What are you doing sneaking up on me like that? You scared me to death!"

He slowly came forward and put his hands on her upper arms, looking into her flushed face. She was shaking violently, and despite the angry words, he didn't think her trembling had anything to do with anger. It was fear. She was rocked to the bone.

"Ashley, what is it? What's got you so frightened?"

She shrugged him off, her breathing still hard. "You. You have me so frightened. Sneaking around in here when I'm trying to close up."

He watched her face. Something else was going on and she was trying to cover it up with bluster.

"Tell me what's going on, Ashley." His voice held the low tone of a man giving a warning. She could storm and rage all she wanted to. He wasn't going to walk away.

She turned her back on him and walked to the circulation desk, picking up her bag and a computer case. She reached into the office behind the desk and flipped off the light before looking at him again.

"Are you coming? I need to lock up."

He stayed where he was and watched her, shaking his head slowly. No, he wasn't coming. He'd wait her out.

"I need to lock up, Garret. The library is closed."

He crossed his arms over his chest and raised a brow. Hell, in all honesty, he wanted to go get an icepack for his jaw. She'd caught him off guard and had clocked him good with that initial blow. But he'd be damned if he'd let her see that.

She changed tactics, her face taking on a wary defensiveness. "What do you want, Garret?"

He stepped closer to her, but kept his hands to himself. He wanted to pull her small body into his, to hold her close and take away whatever fear had spawned that attack. Wanted to, but wouldn't. He didn't know if she was responding to some old fear from a life she'd long left behind, or if this fear was newly kindled. He didn't care. He wanted to put an end to it.

He lowered his voice. "I want to know what has you so on edge. What really has you frightened, because that back there—" He gestured with a shake of his head toward the hallway she'd just attacked him in front of. "That, Ashley, was one of the biggest overreactions I've seen in a long time."

She seemed to break, although it was silent and subtle when she did. The smallest quiver of her lower lip tipped him off, but then she swiped the back of her hand under one eye and took a deep breath. She was mostly composed, with only the slightest bit of fear showing through the façade by the time she spoke.

"Fine. If you must know, someone is playing some kind of stupid joke on me and it has me on edge. I'm sorry. For hitting you, I mean. I shouldn't have done that. I just, I got a little spooked and then I turned that corner and ran into you and I just thought I had to fight back. I thought—"

She broke off, and he didn't want to know what she'd thought. He was filling in the blanks she left with some pretty scary scenarios in his mind. Things he never wanted to think about in relation to Ashley. There were times when being a homicide detective came with a high price. The price of knowing what was out there. Knowing what lurked in the shadows.

And damn, it hit him hard. He did *not* want Ashley meeting any of those things that went bump in the night. The thought of it alone was enough to make his stomach grind.

"What do you mean someone's playing a joke on you? What kind of joke?"

She sighed and looked at her feet for a minute before raising her eyes to meet his. She seemed almost defiant as she told him about finding the rat last night, and then re-finding it this morning. She told him it was nothing. Just teens playing a stupid trick on her, most likely in retaliation for some kind of action she'd taken as librarian.

"I just got spooked tonight. That's all."

Garret didn't like the sound of this at all. A punk teen trying to get even for some small slight at the library wouldn't have hung around and watched her clean up the mess only to retrieve the body and leave it for her again. That brought the whole thing above the level of *prank* in his book.

"I'll follow you home. Take a look at things."

"Really, Garret, that's not necessary." She wrapped her arms around her waist in a protective gesture and he wondered why she felt the need. Was she more worried about this than she was letting on?

"I'd feel better if you'd let me. Please, Ashley?"

She rolled her eyes but didn't object when he followed her out the door and waited as she locked up. As he followed her to her vehicle, his eyes scanned the area. The parking lot was well lit, but she'd parked at the back. He guessed she did that so patrons could take the spots up front, but he didn't like it.

"Ashley, you should park closer to the building." He held up his hand when she opened her mouth, cutting her off before she could object. "I get it. You want to let library patrons have the closer spots. But they aren't coming and going after dark, most of the time."

"This is a quiet town, with very little crime, Garret. I know you see crime over in Branson Falls, but this is Evers. It's not the same here."

He crossed his arms and leveled her with a look. "Wasn't someone attacked in this quiet town of yours a few months ago? Attacked and then kidnapped? Katelyn Bowden, right? Oh, and then there was that shooting out at the Bishop ranch before that? I read the paper, Ashley. I know Evers has its share of crime."

Ashley shook her head and gave him what he was sure was her most pitying look, as if he were a child dreaming of monsters under the bed or goblins in the closet. "Those were isolated incidences with someone who was out to get them."

He raised a brow. "Like the *someone* who left a decapitated rat on your doorstep?"

"That's not the same."

He had to hold in a laugh when she actually stomped her foot at him. "All the same, Ashley, park a little closer." He pointed to a spot that wasn't directly in front of the door but still gave her more light and was very visible from the street. "That spot there gives you the safety you need without taking up a prime spot in front of the door. It's a good compromise."

She rolled her eyes at him again and walked to her car. He gave a quick peek under the car as they approached and looked in through the windows. All clear. Ignoring her laughter at his caution, he opened the door for her, then shut it when she'd slipped in.

"I'll follow you," he said, and went to his car.

As he tailed her home, he began to think of possible scenarios other than a disgruntled teenager. He couldn't help but wonder if a fan had discovered her real name and was focused on her. Or an ex who wasn't happy about the breakup. He wasn't surprised at the way he reacted to that thought. What he was surprised by was the intensity and the visceral level of his response. If it was an ex doing this to her, he wanted to gut the guy. Talk about an overreaction.

The house was mere blocks from the library, on what appeared to be a quiet side road. The houses were small, older bungalows with tidy little yards and single-car garages. Some had only a carport. A few had a child's bike in the yard or a swing tied to a large tree in the front.

Ashley pulled into the driveway of a small yellow house. The paint color was light and cheerful, with clean white shutters and a small white porch. The house had its own unique style, with one side of it made out of corrugated metal flashing. If anyone had described the house to him, he'd have said it would be ugly, but it wasn't. Somehow, it totally worked and made the house stand out.

He pulled over to the curb and parked, getting out and meeting Ashley at the front. She grumbled at him as she unlocked the door.

"I suppose you want me to wait out here while you search the premises. Should I call for backup?"

He looked down at her and had to stifle the urge to haul her smart little ass close to him and kiss the smirk off her face. Damn, there was just something about her when she sassed him. Holy hell, he was in trouble with this woman.

"You're a smart-ass," he said. "I'll settle for you coming in with me while I take a peek around." That wasn't what he wanted at all. He wanted to shut her away in a safe cocoon somewhere while he cleared the house, but he thought she'd go ballistic and kick him out if he tried. He'd take what he could get right now.

He tucked her behind him and tapped his service weapon with his elbow, assuring himself it was there if he needed it. Her front door opened right into the kitchen, followed by an open archway to a living room, with a writing desk and shelves built into the left-hand wall. There were sliding glass doors that led to a fenced backyard. He flicked on the outdoor light and scanned the yard. The light was dim. Not at all what he'd want for her safety.

He returned to the kitchen and followed the single hallway off of it to a small bathroom with bedrooms on either side of it. He quickly checked the rooms. Her bedroom had a door that looked like it might have been original to the house. He guessed the kitchen door that she used as the front door had originally been a side entrance.

"Does this door open?" he asked as he tried the lock.

"No. The previous owners had it sealed and had the door built into the kitchen. It's a strange setup. I actually think at one point the kitchen was the living room and vice versa. Not a clue why they changed it, but I've just left this door sealed up. It's nailed shut and has a couple of coats of paint on the outside, too."

He nodded. "You need better lights outside. And motion sensors to trip them when someone comes on the property. An alarm wouldn't hurt either."

She wrinkled her nose at the idea. "I'll go over to the hardware store and see about motion sensor lights over the weekend, but an alarm is probably more than I need, don't you think?"

He ran a hand over the back of his neck and sighed. "I don't know, Ashley. You tell me. Is there any way this could be a fan? Maybe someone who figured out your real name and is focused on you for some reason? You write some pretty steamy stuff. Has anyone contacted you? Maybe sent you messages online and you haven't responded? Or anyone you've had to block who got a little too personal? Or maybe an ex? Someone around here who might be upset at how things ended?"

She shook her head, but there was a telltale flush to her cheeks. "No exes. I mean, sure, I have exes, but no one I've ended things with in the last year or so. There *was* Pete Masters when I was a junior. I dumped him after we made out behind the bleachers because he kissed like a fish. All tongue and no finesse. Just a lot of slobber. And a lot of tongue. And not tongue in a good way. Tongue in a bad way."

She shook as if a tremor went through her and grinned at him, but he was no longer listening to a damn word she said. He was stuck on kissing. And tongues. Oh, what he wouldn't do to run his tongue from her navel to her neck and back down again. Then, keep on going, right on down to—

"Are you listening to me?"

"No." He answered with the truth. He wasn't listening to a thing she'd said. His cock, however, had stood up at attention and was ready, willing, and able. Not only to listen, but to take direction from this woman. Any direction. She could name it and his dick would jump to it with a "please, may I have another?" Good grief, he was a goner.

Shit. She's still talking. Focus, idiot.

"So I guess someone can technically figure out the person behind the pen name pretty easily. I mean, they wouldn't have to hire a detective to link the books back to me, but I don't advertise the connection in any way."

"Have you had anyone get a little too personal online? Ask questions about your life that go that one step too far? Give you that prickly feeling at the back of your neck?" Good. He was back in the game. Mostly. He shifted slightly, casually trying to relieve the tightness in his jeans. Jeez, she would think he was an ass if she spotted his erection right now.

And there was that telltale flush again.

"All right. Out with it, Ashley. You're blushing any time I ask you if someone got too personal. What is it? What happened?"

She looked at the ground and shrugged. "It's just, um."

She actually shuffled her foot on the floorboards.

"Ashley..." he warned.

"All right," she said, that cute little huffy thing she did with her shoulders coming back. "Some guy sent me a picture of his...of the...of—" She gestured to the general area in front of her hips with her hands and made a funny little noise and blushed a furious shade of red.

"Wait, let me get this straight. You can write a sex scene that takes place in a mountaintop lake in great detail. Right down to the way her muscles clamp down around him as she comes—a sex scene that had me hard for days on end, by the way—but you can't say the word *penis* in a conversation with me?"

Her eyes went wide and she glanced down at his groin, which, thankfully, had settled back down. Not completely, but at least he wasn't sporting something that resembled a tent pole in his pants.

And then it hit him. He processed what she'd said. "Back up. Someone did *what?*"

"Really? You're going to make me say it again? He sent me a full frontal shot of his naked...hip region."

It would have been funny, only it wasn't. "What the hell, Ashley?"

"I know. It happens, though. Some of my friends have had the same thing happen on Facebook. They're friended by someone they think is a fan and then they get a message with a picture. You just unfriend the person, report it, then block them. Problem solved."

"Unless he decided he didn't like your response and he's taken things a step further."

She stepped back, as though he'd frightened her, and he felt a twinge of guilt. But only a twinge. She wasn't taking this as seriously as she should. He stepped closer.

"You need new locks, Ashley. The ones you have aren't nearly good enough. And lights. And an alarm."

"You're scaring me, Garret," she said softly and he backed off a hair.

"Send me the guy's info online so I can have someone track him. I'll see if he's harmless or looks like he might be connected to your rat problem." He paused, then ran one hand up her arm and squeezed gently. What he wanted to do was a lot less gentle, but he'd settled for that. "Okay? Just let me check the guy out."

She nodded.

"Yeah?" he asked again, wanting to be sure she would follow up.

"Yes. I promise," she said, with another nod.

It wasn't until they were walking out of her bedroom to head back to the kitchen that he noticed the other locks. The door to her bedroom had not one, but two deadbolts. And they were heavy duty. The kind he'd like to see on her front and back doors. He wanted to ask her about it, but something told him she wouldn't share that story.

Not yet anyway.

CHAPTER ELEVEN

A shley's phone chirped at six thirty the following day. She didn't have to be at the library until eight in the morning, so six thirty wasn't a time of day she willingly saw. Ever. To say she wasn't a morning person was putting it mildly.

She reached one hand out from under the blanket, being sure to keep it over her head. Keeping her head covered so she didn't see the rising sun would be crucial to going back to sleep once she was sure the text wasn't an emergency.

The light from the screen lit the text well enough that she could make it out under the blanket.

If you hear a noise don't panic. It's just me.

Ashley sat up in bed, covers falling to her waist in a puddle. Garret?

What?

I'm outside. I'll start on outside lights. Do the inside stuff later.

The man made no sense.

What?

When in doubt, repeat the same question until you get an answer that makes sense. Sure. That was a good strategy.

Really? he texted back.

Okay, she probably deserved that. Before she could text back, he called.

"What are you doing outside my house?" She didn't bother with a greeting. If he wanted a greeting, he should have led with coffee instead of cryptic texts, and he should have shown up at least an hour later. Six thirty. What was the man thinking?

"I'm outside. I've got lights and locks. I'll start out here."

She hung up the phone and stared blankly at her wall. Garret Hensley was outside her house. Installing lights. She debated her options. Make coffee. Go say hello. Go back to bed.

She looked at herself in the mirror that hung over her makeup table. Her bark of laughter at her reflection probably wasn't very ladylike. Whatever. He could wait.

She fell back on her pillow, drew the covers over her head, and tried to go back to sleep. In all likelihood, she'd just dreamed the whole thing anyway. Besides, she was still pretty annoyed with herself for how she acted around him. She was known for having very few inhibitions and for speaking her mind without filtering her thoughts.

But yesterday, she'd turned into a blushing schoolgirl

when she'd tried to explain that she'd gotten pictures of a guy's penis in her inbox. What the heck was that about? She could say penis 'til the cows came home. *Penis, penis, penis. Cock, dick, wanker, one-eyed-snake, chubby, fire hose, ramrod, pleasure pole, meat missile, midnight wrangler, mister happy, wacker, wang, wee-wee, willy.* Yup. She was good with talking about the penis. So why on earth had she clammed up in front of Garret?

Ugh. Now she lay in her bed, with the man outside her house, as she daydreamed about what *his* sexy-stick might look like. What it might feel like.

Ugh.

GARRET TRIED to wipe the grin off his face, but he had a feeling he didn't do a very good job of it. He'd catch hell from the guys if he walked into the station like this, but he couldn't help himself. He'd spent an hour putting up solar-powered, motion-triggered floodlights outside Ashley's house. Then, because he'd discovered through his earlier texts and phone calls that she didn't function well early in the morning, he had gone into town and bought her a coffee and chocolate croissant from the bakery.

The first grin had appeared on his face when she hung up on him. The second when she slammed the door in his face. He wasn't sure if it was the slamming door or the way her hair stood wildly on end as though she'd slept in a wind tunnel. But he didn't care. He knocked again, calling out that he had coffee and chocolate, and the door had opened immediately.

"I brought locks for the windows and doors, too. And door guards to help prevent the locks from being jimmied. I can install them while you drink that," he said with a nod to the coffee he handed her. She grunted at him. Grunted. Not a cute delicate ladylike noise. A real, full-on, man-sized grunt.

He laughed. Then he installed the locks, door guards, and window locks. His third big grin had come when she reappeared, showered and dressed and no longer grunting. She had smiled then, and thanked him. And she'd let him walk her to work. Then she'd let him kiss her goodbye outside the library doors at eight thirty in the morning. That had been his final big grin. Final because the damn thing still hadn't left his fool face.

He couldn't get it out of his head. It would have been perfect if all she had done was let him kiss her. It would have been perfect even then, because the scent of her shampoo filled him, dizzying him with its floral potion. It would have been perfect if all he had gotten from her was the tiny sigh she'd let out as she leaned into him, letting her stomach and chest brush his body, starting flames he had a hard time putting to rest.

But she took it a damn sight further when she trailed one hand up the nape of his neck and twisted her fingers into his hair, pulling his head down to her. Pulling him into the kiss. Deeper. Longer. Harder.

It was one hell of a grin-inducing, body-hardening kiss.

And he planned to relive it every minute of every hour of the day today. *Screw it.* The guys could say whatever the hell they wanted. He wasn't about to wipe that fool look off his face for shit.

"My office, Hensley!"

Well, that lasted all of two minutes. One foot in the door and his captain was bellowing for him already. He hadn't cursed, so with any luck that just meant he'd taken a message or had a lead he wanted Garret to chase down for him. He needed a lead right about now. He hadn't gotten back anything from the lab that would help track Alice's killer, and his frustration was grating on him.

Normally, he was all right with the process. Making the phone calls, doing the interviews, chasing one little thread of the case at a time. But when the case involved the death of a friend—no, family—he wasn't able to handle things as calmly as he should.

Doug was already in the room, and Garret had a quick flash of unease as he wondered if his captain had found out about his connection to Alice. He would probably be pulled off, and might even lose his job if his captain found out. But he kept his mouth shut and waited. He wasn't going to say anything until he was sure the captain knew something.

Captain Sharp watched him over steepled fingers for more than a few minutes. Garret kept his face carefully blank and made sure not to catch his partner's eye. If it came down to it, he'd swear up and down Doug knew nothing about his connection to Alice. He'd protect his partner.

"Why do I get the feeling you're not telling me something, Hensley?" His captain's eyes drilled into him, but he schooled his features and affected a careless face.

"Not sure what you're talking about, Cap. I got nothing to hide."

His captain grunted, but lifted a folder from his desk and tossed it to them. Garret grabbed the toss and flipped open the folder. It was a file from social services. Bill and Tanya Franks. He didn't connect it to any case right off the bat. Until he saw a name that told him exactly what and who this was connected to.

"What's this?" Garret asked, handing the file to Doug. He saw the moment Doug froze. It was only a split second before the seasoned cop shook off his surprise. But Garret knew he'd seen the same thing Garret had spotted. In the file marked Bill and Tanya Franks—whoever the hell they were—was Ashley's name. Front and center.

His captain didn't seem to catch the change in either man; instead he answered Garret's question. "This is a file Alice Johnson asked an intern at social services to dig up for her a few days before she was killed. The intern forgot about it until someone from records sent it over this morning. She brought it by, thinking it might help you trace what Alice was working on."

Doug tapped the file on his knee, all business. "Great. We'll run it down. See where it leads."

Garret nodded and stood, only to have the captain stop them both. "Are you sure you don't want to share anything, gentlemen? If I find out you're hiding anything from me, I can't promise I'll have your backs. I can only protect you if you trust me."

Doug shook his head, slowly, his mouth pulled down at the sides. "Nothing to protect us from, Cap. Nothing at all."

Garret felt a pain lance through his gut and realized it was guilt. He shouldn't have dragged Doug into this. But what other choice had he had? He needed to find Alice's killer. There was no way he'd trust anyone else to do it. The department wasn't big and the two other detective teams had a lot less experience than he and Doug had. One pair had worked one homicide in the past and the other had worked two. That hardly stacked up against the experience he and Doug had handling ten homicides and umpteen other violent crimes over the years.

No. There was no way he could entrust this case to anyone else. When his captain nodded, he walked out of the room alongside his partner and hoped the shit didn't spray too damn far when it hit the proverbial fan.

CHAPTER TWELVE

Ashley felt like she did back in high school when Jake Kimball kissed her behind the bleachers. It wasn't that he was the captain of the football team. And it wasn't that everyone liked him. And it wasn't that he had jet-black hair and black-as-night eyes that she could feel on her whenever he looked at her during class.

It was the way he stood close enough for her to feel the strength of his body barely brushing against hers. It was the way her breath caught when he leaned in close as she closed her eyes and hoped for a kiss. And it was the way she felt giddy any time she thought of him and that kiss.

Garret's kiss this morning had been so much more enticing than Jake's. Which made sense, given that she and Jake had been teens. But still. The kiss this morning had been in a whole other league altogether. She could still feel her toes curling, her heart racing, and that flutter in her stomach. All from a simple kiss.

She'd tried not to let herself fantasize about what else she and Garret could do if they made it to a bed, but she was a romance novelist, after all. Scenes had been racing through her mind at utterly inappropriate times all day. She was fairly sure she'd moaned out loud at one point when Mrs. Shacklemire was standing next to the circulation desk. She'd faked a pain in her neck and shrugged it off, but she was sure Mr. Shacklemire would get an earful about it when the Mrs. got home. Then he'd go down to Jansen's Feed Store, and sure enough the story would be out before the end of the day.

It wouldn't be the first time Ashley would be the subject of town gossip. She'd grabbed the Queen of Town Talk title early on when she'd arrived in town and she hadn't given it up too frequently over the years. She smiled to herself and shrugged off the concern. She had tough skin where gossip was concerned. She could deal with it.

Until she saw the look on Garret's face when he walked in that afternoon. It was apologetic. And something else. Determined? Haunted? There were so many emotions, Ashley couldn't read them all and she had to fight the sudden urge to flee.

His partner, Doug, whom she'd met on only one occasion earlier, lurked in the background as Ashley's thoughts began to swirl. If he was here to tell her he regretted the kiss, he wouldn't bring his partner, would he? Then again, maybe he might? Maybe he wanted his partner here so she wouldn't cause a scene? Did he really think she was that kind of woman? Actually, wait. Maybe she *was* that kind of woman.

He took a step forward and lowered his voice, even though the library was quiet now. The quilters were in the activity room, but they kept the door shut so they could chat while they worked without bothering the library patrons.

"Can we talk in your office, Ashley?"

"Sure," she said, trying to keep her voice light. She was pretty sure it didn't work.

He shut the door after they walked into her office, and the small space and closeness of their bodies didn't affect her the way it had that morning. She just felt edgy and uneasy and a little like she might throw up.

He raised his hand, and it was then that she realized he was holding a folder. "I need to know about Bill Franks, Ashley."

She took two steps back, her arms wrapped around her stomach. The blow was visceral, kicking her in the gut. She tried to take a deep breath and battle the tears that pricked behind her eyes, but she was losing the battle.

"Hey, hey." His voice was a gentle croon, but she still shook her head at him and tried to back away farther. She couldn't think about Bill Franks. Couldn't talk about him. She simply couldn't. That part of her life was over and she wouldn't go back there. Not for anything.

The fact that her present was colliding with horrible past made her sick to her stomach.

"Ashley, I need you to tell me what happened in that

house. I need to know why Alice would pull this file right before she was killed."

His words were enough to snap Ashley back to the present, but she wasn't able to face him as the woman she was today. As the woman she had been that morning. She felt the hardened shield she'd worn as a mantle during her teen years come down over her once more. She saw it reflected in his eyes and knew he'd seen the change.

To his credit, he didn't react. His eyes maintained their steady gaze.

"Not a damn thing happened that matters now. Alice got me out. She pulled his license. That's all that matters. He doesn't have kids in the house." She said that as a statement, but in her heart, it was a plea. A silent but powerful plea, because God, he could *not* have kids in that house.

When Garret spoke, he did so quietly. Deliberately. "I don't have any reason to think he has kids there, but I'll find out for sure. I just need to know what Alice was doing. I need to know if this might be a lead in her case. You need to tell me why she would have pulled the file."

She shut off all emotion. Everything. She barely saw the man in front of her. "I have no idea why Alice would be looking at that file. There can't be kids there. There are no kids there."

Garret questioned her a little longer, but she couldn't tell him anything else. When he left, she gathered her things and asked the part-time assistant and the afternoon volunteer if they'd mind closing up for her. She begged off as sick, and they didn't question it. After assuring them she didn't need a ride home, she walked out of the library and went straight home. She was trying to outrun her ghosts, and she honestly wasn't sure she'd be able to run fast or far enough.

DOUG PULLED up across from the tire and brake center where Bill Franks worked and shut off the engine of the unmarked cruiser. Garret checked his watch. It was almost six o'clock.

"Let's hold off on a visit to the workplace and just see where this guy goes when he gets off. I'm less concerned about what we might find when we talk to his boss than what we might find at his house," Doug said. As usual, he and his partner were on the same page. Working with someone new when Doug retired would be a bitch.

"Yeah." Garret nodded. "I doubt anything he's doing at a tire and brake shop would have drawn Alice's attention. Ashley didn't say much, but it's clear this guy shouldn't be around kids. My money says Alice spotted him with a kid somewhere, or found out he has a kid in his home. We need to figure out what she saw."

Doug nodded. Justice for the dead drove them. But even more so, protecting children would always be at the forefront of their work. If Alice truly believed a child was in danger, she would have acted on that belief. Garret knew Doug was wondering the same thing he was. If that need to protect was what got Alice killed. And if there was a child out there in danger.

The men waited in their vehicle until twenty past the hour, when they spotted a man matching the DMV photo they had of Bill Franks leave the shop. He got into an older sedan and pulled out of the lot. They followed shortly in their unmarked car. Doug stayed well behind, tailing at a discreet distance. It wasn't difficult, since it appeared Franks was headed to the address they had on file for him.

Ten minutes later, they pulled alongside the curb outside a small house in a lower-class neighborhood. It wasn't the worst of the worst as far as neighborhoods went. But the houses were small and many weren't kept up the way they ought to be. Fresh paint was in short supply and cars were all older models. There were teenagers hanging out on the corners and Garret would bet they weren't doing anything legal.

"Car thefts?" Garret asked, receiving an answering nod from Doug.

The two men exited the vehicle and approached Franks' front door. They didn't need to talk about how the following few minutes would go. They'd done this dozens of times.

When they knocked on the door of number 1872 moments later, they heard a man yell for someone to get the damned door. A woman with long black hair opened it with a smile on her face. She was in the middle of laughing and tossing an "I'm gettin' it, I'm gettin' it" over her shoulder. Her voice held more humor than the man's voice had, as if she were somehow charmed by his foul mood.

"Hello, gentlemen." There was a flirty nature to her tone and her body language followed suit. She leaned into the doorframe as she smiled up at them. "What can I do for you?"

"Ma'am," Doug said, with a nod and a flash of his badge. "We're investigation a string of break-ins in the neighborhood. Cars being rifled through. DVDs, electronics coming up missing."

In reality, two detectives wouldn't be canvassing a neighborhood over missing DVDs, but no one ever seemed to catch on to that fact. Garret and Doug had used this ruse whenever they needed a peek inside a house or needed to talk to someone without raising suspicions. People fell for it every time.

"Who's'it?" Bill Franks asked as he came up behind the woman, turning three words into one. He grabbed her ass, seemingly without concern for the fact that anyone was witnessing his action. Or maybe it was for their benefit.

Doug repeated the bit for Bill Franks, while Garret casually scanned the inside of the living room. Not much was visible from where they stood, but he didn't spot any sign of a child. No toys, at least. No child-sized shoes or so much as a hoodie tossed on the couch.

"Huh," Franks said as he scratched his chest. "Ain't had any trouble here. I got a big spotlight in the driveway at night. Neighbor bitches about it, but no one's gonna mess with my shit with all that light."

"I haven't seen anyone around any cars." The woman smiled again. Damn, her jaw looked like it might break if she didn't quit that.

Garret began to shift back and forth on his feet, fidgeting openly.

"What the hell, er, uh—heck—sorry, ma'am. What the heck is the matter with you?" Doug asked, turning to Garret.

Garret did his best to look sheepish as he glanced at Franks and the woman, then back to Doug. Sheepish wasn't an easy look for him, but he made it work when he had to. "I need to use the can. We've been out here a long time knockin' on doors." Another quick glance at the woman.

She bought it, opening the door wide. "Come on in, officer. You can use our bathroom."

Franks gave her a hard look, but didn't argue. He stepped back and let the men in. After Franks waved Garret down the hall to a small half bath, Doug began to ask questions about how Franks installed his spotlight in the driveway, chatting him up and stroking his ego. It kept Franks' focus on Doug as Garret peeked into doors and checked out the kitchen, what looked like a ground-level master bedroom, and a den.

There wouldn't be an easy way to get upstairs without arousing suspicion, but Garret hadn't seen any sign of a child. They needed to withdraw and take another tack.

"All set, Doug," he said, coming back into the living room where the group stood. "Thank you for letting me use your bathroom. We still have to cover all the other houses on this street. You guys just saved me a pretty uncomfortable evening."

After an appropriate round of goodbyes, during which Doug instructed the couple to call him if they saw anything suspicious, Garret and Doug walked out to the sidewalk.

"Anything?" Doug asked.

"No toys or clothes. No drawings or family shots on the fridge. Nothing. I didn't get a look upstairs, obviously, but I didn't see anything that says there's a kid in that house. You get the woman's name?"

Doug nodded. "Michelle Davis. Live-in girlfriend. Let's check with a few of the neighbors to be sure. Can't hurt to let them think we're out here questioning people about car break-ins. Keep up our story in case we need to come back."

But an hour later, they'd only turned up plenty of neighbors who apparently kept their heads in the sand and knew next to nothing about the people living around them. One woman said she thought the girlfriend was a new addition. That she'd only been around for the last month or so. She wasn't sure if she had a child, but thought maybe she did.

Garret rubbed his forehead with his thumb and forefinger, trying to force the strain from his head.

"We need to find out where the wife went." The file Alice had pulled indicated a wife lived with him back when he'd been an approved foster parent.

"I'll run a search on her in the morning," Doug said. "See if she's deceased or if they divorced. If he was up to what we suspect, it's possible she left him. Maybe she found out and didn't want to live with a pedophile."

Garret nodded. He hadn't seen any sign of a child in the home, but his gut was screaming at him. He'd bet his signed Mickey Mantle baseball card that this case was the reason Alice was dead. He just needed to find out why.

CHAPTER THIRTEEN

"Tell me why I haven't been hearing from you," Cora said, taking Ashley's hand in hers as the two women walked from the library to the diner. Ashley couldn't blame her sister for asking. They usually spoke every day, but Ashley had been avoiding Cora for the last few days. She didn't want to tell anyone what was going on. She didn't want to admit that she'd been slipping back into the darkest days of her life. Days she thought she had left behind.

"I've been busy," she said. "The library has a new software system going in and I have to update all the computers and get the whole catalogue transitioned over. It's a big project."

Cora narrowed her eyes. "Try again. That was last month and you're almost finished."

Ashley rolled her eyes and feigned annoyance. "There were a few bugs. I'm working with the software company's rep to figure them out."

It wasn't entirely a lie, just an *almost* one. She was, in fact, almost finished with the whole transition, bugs and all. But Cora didn't need to know that. She didn't need to know that Ashley had been unable to sleep and wasn't eating much. She didn't need to know that the life Ashley never imagined she could have was now slipping away. That she was drowning in the memories of what had once almost taken her down. That this time she wasn't sure she could tread water long enough to reach safety.

"Who is she, Mommy?" Evie lifted her head from the coloring pages her teacher had printed on the computer for her. She knew it was a risk asking her mother about the pretty lady they'd been watching, but she was tired. Making her mother angry might just get her to take them home. Evie wanted to go back to her room. She wanted to be able to eat her snack and color her pages.

"Who is who?" Her mother's voice was sharp, but she didn't move her eyes from the window as she watched the two women cross the street. It wasn't the taller woman they were watching. She'd only just arrived. It was the one with the long hair. The one who looked like the porcelain dolls Evie had once seen in a shop window when they'd lived in a big city a long time ago. Dallas, she thought it was called. She wasn't really sure. But the sound of Dallas was nice.

"The doll lady." She didn't look up from her coloring page.

"The doll lady?" Her mother mimicked back to her. "What doll lady? I don't see a doll."

"She looks like a doll," Evie said, head ducked.

Her mother didn't answer. She started the car and drove away. Evie smiled to herself as she finished filling in the yellow duck on her page. She would work on the umbrella next. She wanted to color it purple. Or maybe sky blue. The colored pencils her teacher had bought for her were her most treasured possession. She was risking them by using them in front of her mother. When Michelle got angry, she sometimes lashed out by taking whatever she knew to be most prized by Evie at the time. But they had been in the car for hours that afternoon. Evie was tired and hungry, and she'd been bored until she pulled the coloring pages and pencils out. With any luck, her mother wouldn't notice them.

She slid the pages and pencils back in her bag and zipped it up. Letting her forehead fall to the window, she watched as they drove past the doll lady and her tall friend. The doll lady was talking to her friend and didn't look at them as they drove past, but Evie could see her eyes for the first time. They were the bluest eyes she'd ever seen. But they were also sad eyes. She hadn't expected the doll to be sad. Somehow, that didn't seem right.

CHAPTER FOURTEEN

"**D**amn it!" Garret slammed the phone back into its cradle on the corner of his desk, coming close to knocking it clear off. Doug raised his brows at his partner, but remained silent.

Garret expelled a harsh breath, trying to rein in his frustration before speaking. He took another breath before looking up at his partner. "No DNA results yet, and so far, there isn't any blood type other than Alice's at the scene. It's possible she and the killer share the same type and we'll get more detailed analysis later with the DNA, but..."

"Yeah, and I wear Prada in my off hours," said Doug, finishing the thought for Garret. Of course, Garret wouldn't have said it in quite the same way, but the point was made. He was tempted to ask how Doug even knew what the hell Prada was, but his mood was too foul to bother. He continued to rattle off the report he'd just been given instead.

"They've got a partial print that doesn't match Alice's, but it's not enough to run. There's nothing else. Nothing other than the file Alice asked for. Which means we're back to squat."

Doug shook his head and sighed. Garret knew both the look and the sound. Something was coming that he didn't want to hear, and he knew damn well what it was.

"Don't say it."

"I've gotta say it, Garret, and you know I do. We need to push Ashley. She's not telling you everything, and there's something there. I can feel it and I know damned well you can feel it."

"She said the guy couldn't have a kid in the home. That's enough to tell me what happened years ago. I don't need that shit spelled out for me any more than she needs to spell it out. There wasn't a kid there that you and I could see. Maybe Alice thought there was, but she was wrong."

As he said the words, they needled at him. Would Alice have contacted Ashley if she thought there was any chance she was wrong about a child? No. But that didn't mean she wasn't wrong. They hadn't found any evidence of a child in the home. Maybe whatever Alice thought she'd uncovered simply wasn't there.

They'd run the report on Franks' wife and she'd died years before of natural causes. Breast cancer that hadn't been caught until it was much too late to do anything more than try to keep her comfortable.

"Garret, I've backed you on this so far, but it's time. We need to lean on Ashley. I'll do it if you want me to. I'll be as

118

gentle as I can, but we have to do this, partner. You know we do."

Garret ground his teeth together and fought for some shred of an argument against the logic laid out before him. There wasn't anything, though. He knew Doug was right. It had to be done.

"I'll do it," he said, trying not to let the words come out harshly. He met his partner's eyes. "I'll do it."

GARRET RAISED his hand and rang the bell once again, glancing toward Ashley's car in the driveway and back to the door. He'd thought initially she might have gone out for a walk or with a friend who'd picked her up. He knew the library was closed today, being a Sunday. So he had walked into town and grabbed a sandwich for lunch. He hadn't felt much like eating since he'd had that talk with Doug the previous day, but he forced a sandwich down by force of habit.

He had arrived back at Ashley's a few minutes ago and begun ringing the bell, alternating with banging on the door. He didn't know what told him she was in there. Hell, he was likely wrong. She had said she often went to her parent's place for dinner on Sundays. Maybe she'd gone over early today?

Damn. He walked back to his car, gut eating at him. Doug had been right. He needed to question Ashley. He should have pushed her on this long before. He pulled out the file he kept on her, the one that he'd started the minute she'd walked into the case. It didn't go very deep, but he had her phone number and the names of her parents and siblings in it. He'd tried her number several times already. It was going straight to voicemail.

On a whim, he looked up her sister's name and pulled the phone number. He knew she was close to Cora. Cora would know where he could find her. He wasn't sure if he was going to such great lengths because he thought he should question her as soon as possible, or if he was listening to the needling worry at the back of his mind.

"Cora?"

"Yes?" Her answer was slow and questioning, reflecting the fact that she wasn't sure about answering a call from a blocked number.

"My name is Detective Garret Hensley from the Branson Falls Police Department. I'm trying to reach your sister, Ashley, to follow up with her, and wondered if she was with you."

There was silence on the line. Okay, so the woman probably didn't get calls from detectives trying to track her sister often. And really, when had he ever made a call like this on a case? He hadn't. Because if he was honest with himself, he wasn't calling for the case. He was calling because he wanted to see Ashley.

He cleared his throat. "Ashley said she sometimes eats dinner at your parents' house on Sundays, but her car is in the driveway, so I thought you might have picked her up? Or maybe one of your other siblings?" He knew he sounded stiff and forced, but he was trying to show her Ashley had trusted him with personal information. What he said had caught her attention, though.

"Her car is there? But she isn't answering the door?" There was a hint of suspicion in her tone. And something else. Maybe surprise? "Can I call you right back?"

He rattled off his number and the line was disconnected. He looked at the phone, and if he had to guess, he'd bet Cora was trying to call Ashley. Within moments, he received a text from the number he'd just dialed to reach Cora. *On my way there.*

Now he was concerned. Cora wouldn't rush right over if she didn't think something was wrong, would she? No, she wouldn't. He was sure of it.

Garret stepped from his car and crossed the yard to the porch. To hell with it. He pulled the small set of tools he kept in his wallet for "emergencies" and went to work. Damn. He'd almost forgotten he had put some pretty foolproof locks on the doors the other day. They weren't as easy to jimmy as he'd like, but he was able to get in after a few minutes. The lights were off, but he called out.

"Ashley! Are you here? It's Garret. Cora's on her way." He flipped on the lights in the living room and looked around. He didn't see anything out of place. Nothing out of the ordinary. So why the hell was his gut screaming at him so damned loudly? If there wasn't anything wrong, he'd feel like a Peeping Tom, but he needed to know she was safe. Hopefully she wasn't just an unusually heavy sleeper taking a nap in the next room. That would sure as hell suck. How would he live down the creepy stalker image that would imprint in her head?

"Ashley?" he called out again. This time, he heard a whimper. It was small, but it was enough to chill his blood and send his hand to the holster at his side. His thumb remained on the grip of his firearm, ready to draw if needed. He cleared the kitchen and living room with a glance, and proceeded down the hallway toward Ashley's room. The bedroom lights were on when he entered, but there was no sign of Ashley.

He stood still and listened. A sob. The closet.

Garret opened the closet door and took in the sight before him. Ashley curled in a ball on the floor in the far corner of the small walk-in closet. She was huddled, knees to chest, tears streaming down her face. His hand left his holster and he swept her frame as he moved to kneel in front of her.

No sign of injury or assault. Clothing intact.

"Ashley, are you okay?" *Dumbass.* Who asks a woman who's so clearly not okay if they're okay?

He very slowly moved his hand to her arm. She had her eyes open, but he wasn't sure she saw him, because she jumped and began to shake her head back and forth, squeezing her eyes shut. He'd had a lot of experience as a cop. Dealt with a lot. But he felt far out of his depth right now.

He backed off but stayed close, watching, talking. "Cora is coming, Ashley. She's on her way. I'll stay here with you until she gets here. I'm not going to hurt you, but I also don't want to leave you alone, okay? I'll just stay right here. Cora's coming." He repeated his words over and over as she continued to shake her head.

He'd never felt so useless or so relieved when he heard the front door open. "In here," he called out as softly as he could. Cora and Laura, who he'd met with Ashley in front of the diner, rounded the corner into the room. He slowly backed out of the closet and stood to the side and watched, hands shoved in his pockets, as they helped Ashley to her feet and brought her to her bed.

There would be no asking her anything tonight, but he still felt like he needed to do something, *anything*, for her. Only what could he do? What he wanted to do was head for his car, drive straight to Bill Franks' house, and put a bullet through the man's head. Because he had no doubt that whatever had caused this incredibly strong woman to melt before him had begun with that man.

"Thank you, detective. We'll take it from here," Cora said, not sparing him a glance as she wrapped Ashley in a quilt. Laura had climbed right up onto the bed with Ashley and had her arms wrapped around her, talking quietly in her ear.

Garret warred with himself. He wanted to stay. To do something to help. But he also knew in his heart Ashley would hate for him to be here. Hate for him to see her like this.

"It's all right, Detective. We've got it," Cora prompted again.

He nodded. "Can I call you later to check on her?"

Cora offered him a small smile and a nod. "Sure. Thank you. You can let yourself out?" She phrased it as a question, but he recognized it for the dismissal it was. He took one last look at the tiny woman on the bed, still curled on her side, her breath hitching in big gulps as she stared sightlessly at the wall beside her. Then he walked away, determined to figure out the secret that had killed Alice and was tearing the woman he had begun to feel some pretty strong things for apart. There was something out there, and he needed to uncover it.

CHAPTER FIFTEEN

Ashley didn't know how long she slept. When she woke, Cora and Laura were on either side of her. They smiled down at her, but she could see the worry in their eyes. If there were ever two women who knew what she was going through, it was them. There wasn't any judgment. They didn't look at her like she was a freak. They were simply concerned. And she got that. It had been a hell of a meltdown.

And then she remembered someone else's concerned eyes. Garret's. *Oh God*. Garret had seen her. So much for pretending she was a normal, sane person. Ashley pressed her lips tightly together and blinked. She wouldn't cry again. She was cried out. But damn, it sucked to feel the hard-fought life she'd built slipping away from her. She felt like she was standing on the edge of a cliff, with the rock face crumbling beneath her bit by bit. No matter how far she backpedaled, the crumbling earth would sweep her away in its wake. It would always be faster than she was.

She took a deep breath and rolled her eyes. "I bet I look gorgeous," she said with a watery smile. "It's my new look. I'm calling it swollen puffy girl."

Laura laughed. "You forgot about your hair. It's more like swollen puffy girl with hair standing on end." She tilted her head. "Somehow you're making it work for you. Pretty disgusting, if you ask me."

Cora groaned. "Ash could look gorgeous in a hurricane with clown makeup on. It's just not fair."

"I had to chase away the hot detective somehow. I'm pretty sure I got the job done with this scene, huh?" She all but flinched as she thought again about him witnessing this meltdown. It was mortifying. Talk about damaged goods.

"Now, why would you want to chase away that hot man? Besides, he wanted to hang around and help, so I'm pretty sure you haven't succeeded yet. I thought I was going to have to shove him out the door," Cora said.

"Ha! I'm sure it was like watching a train wreck. Who could look away?"

Laura spoke gently. "Why would you want to chase him away, Ashley? Seems to me, the man would be a pretty great catch. You sure you want to push him out of your life before you've given him a chance?"

Ashley didn't answer. What was there to say? She was having flashbacks of epic proportions. And even before that, she hadn't been sure she would be able to build a life with someone. Now? It seemed out of the question. She'd been on her closet floor huddled in a ball, pretty much catatonic. Who would want *that*?

Never mind if he found out why. No man would want a relationship with a woman like her.

Sure, she'd had relationships with guys. But they were sexual relationships. When she'd realized she couldn't force intimacy and closeness through sex, she'd also begun to believe she might never be able to find the real thing. Because once a guy found out the truth about her, how could he possibly want to be with her in any way other than sexually? He couldn't. It was as simple as that.

But she didn't say any of that to Laura and Cora.

Laura narrowed eyes that saw too much and looked at Ashley.

"Do you remember when you told me that maybe it was time for me to stop running? To give this place a chance?"

Ashley nodded, not sure where Laura was going with this. She'd stopped running a long time ago. It was why she had her family and her friends and her career. Because she'd given Evers and the Walkers a chance. Despite everything she'd been through, she *had* stopped running.

Cora took Ashley's hand in hers and held it as Laura spoke.

"I wouldn't have the life I've been able to build here if I hadn't listened to you. I wouldn't have a husband who loves me and treasures me, and a beautiful child to love; a family and friends."

Ashley didn't answer, but that didn't stop Laura. "You might think you stopped running when you arrived here. When your family took you in, when they adopted you. You think you stopped running and gave them a chance."

Now Ashley opened her mouth to speak, but Laura held up her hand. Her eyes were soft but she was shaking her head at Ashley. "Let me finish, Ash. You stopped running to some extent. But you've held a part of you locked away for a long time. There's a piece of you that never faced what happened. I'm willing to bet you've never even told your mom or Cora what it is. And that piece of you is still running. You won't ever be whole until you truly stop and face it head-on with open eyes. And I think you deserve to be whole. To live a full life with someone you love, who you allow to love you back. You deserve that in your world, Ashley."

But Ashley didn't answer. She closed her eyes, because she knew the truth. She didn't deserve that. And if any of them knew the truth about what happened years ago, they would know she didn't deserve that. She couldn't ever have love and children of her own, the way that Laura had. The way her parents had. That was something she'd given up the right to years ago. And there was no going back and undoing what she'd done.

Garret texted Doug to let him know he hadn't been able to talk to Ashley yet, but he'd follow up again tomorrow. He needed to do something, though. He couldn't just sit and twiddle his damned thumbs while he waited for something to turn up in this case. He needed to dig up a witness to talk to, a thread to pull, some small trail or lead to follow. Alice's case was quickly turning cold, and he owed her a hell of a lot more than that.

His mind was on Alice and all the times she'd made him iced tea as he sat at her kitchen table while his mom worked. She'd always talked to him like he was a grown up, even when he'd been eight or nine or ten. She'd talked to him as though he were intelligent, worthy of her attention. As though he could be or do anything.

He played back the memories of her talks as he steered his car back toward the one lead he had in the case. Bill Franks' house. Pulling over, he cut the engine and watched the house from down the street. He'd sit here all day if he had to. Until Ashley was in any kind of shape to tell him what he needed to know, he'd watch and wait.

The night passed by and Garret sat, watching silently, without the urge to sleep. He got this way on cases when things began to come to a boil. As morning broke and the neighborhood started to come to life with people headed to work or school or places unknown, he spotted them. The woman he'd met at Franks' place the other day came out of the house and headed to a car. Only this time, she wasn't alone. She had a young girl in tow. A girl with a backpack almost as big as her tiny frame, and clothes that looked to be a size too small. As Garret watched, the two left the house and drove away. Away from the home of Bill Franks.

A man Garret very strongly suspected had a taste for young girls.

He let out a string of curses and started the car. He knew in his gut this was what Alice had died doing. She died trying to get that kid out of that home. He'd not only finish the job, he'd bring her killer down.

Ready or not, Ashley had to talk to him. It was time.

CHAPTER SIXTEEN

Cora answered the door when Garret arrived at Ashley's house an hour and a half later. He hadn't showered or shaved, and he was sure his clothes were rumpled. Based on the look on Cora's face, she was gearing up to fend him off, to try to convince him to leave her sister alone. God, how he'd give anything to do just that. But that wasn't going to happen. Couldn't happen. Not now that he knew there was a child in the home with Bill Franks.

He'd called Doug to report in, but convinced his partner to let him come see Ashley alone. To give her that much privacy while she told him what he needed to know. He'd get one shot at this and one shot only. If he didn't get answers now, Doug wouldn't give him any more slack. And Garret wouldn't blame him.

He spoke before Cora could. "It's time, Cora. I need to speak with her. Now."

She looked at him for a long time, and he debated

pulling his badge and forcing the issue. He heard the soft murmur of Ashley's voice behind her. With a relenting sigh, Cora let the door swing open and stepped aside. Ashley sat in sweatpants and a worn tee on the couch. Her hands hugged a mug of something hot and her face was scrubbed clean of makeup and tears. She looked...not refreshed...but a bit rested. Like she'd had time to get her bearings.

He didn't waste any time. He sat on the coffee table in front of her, assuming a familiarity not normally taken in this kind of situation, but one he would take with Ashley. She didn't object. He just hoped after all this was over, she'd give him a shot with her. He liked this woman a lot. He respected the hell out of her. She was intelligent and strong and so damned sexy he felt like he needed a cold shower every time he got within a few yards of her. Touching distance. Smelling distance. Those were the things that doomed him with this woman.

"There's a child in his house, Ashley. I don't know who she is yet. I suspect his girlfriend's daughter."

Ashley went sheet-white in an instant and Cora sat by her side. Ashley began to scratch at her arms, and for the first time Garret noticed thin white scars like train tracks on her forearms. Cutting. They were old scars, but they told the story of someone trying to outrun pain. A lot of it.

Cora took Ashley's hand in hers and held tight while Garret went on.

"She's not much younger than you were when you were taken out of the home. I suspect Alice thought she had a little time until she reached Bill Franks' preferred age. She's nine, maybe ten. But there isn't much time, Ashley. I need the story. I need something to give me the leverage I need to get in there and get that kid out. If my instincts are right, when Alice showed up asking questions, Bill Franks got nervous and fought back."

Ashley lowered her head, her eyes squeezing shut for the briefest of moments. When she raised her head again and looked him in the eye, he saw nothing but steel. Steely determination to do what had to be done. And God, he wanted to pull her close and tell her she didn't need to do it. She didn't have to go through this. But he couldn't do that. Couldn't protect her, because protecting her—letting her off the hook—might leave that little girl in danger.

The words that came out of her mouth rocked him to the core. And that was something he never thought could happen. In a shaking voice, she told him what he needed to know.

"Behind the garage, on the left side, there's a small carving of an angel. Dig there. Test the DNA. You'll find mine and his. That's all you'll need." Tears began to stream down her face, and God help him, he wanted to pull her into his arms and hold her. He wanted to make this go away for her.

He inhaled a steadying breath. He and Cora both looked at Ashley, and from the look on Cora's face, she was struggling to process what she had said just as much as he was.

She couldn't possibly mean...

"Ashley," he said, swallowing hard. "You were fourteen

when you were taken out of that home."

"Yes."

Cora's eyes met his. "Ashley, do you mean—"

His mind reeled. What could she mean? Had she buried evidence of sexual assault? Clothing or bedding with bodily fluids? The thought made his stomach lurch. What came next hit him even harder. He never saw it coming.

Ashley averted her eyes like she couldn't face him. "A baby. I hid it for a long time. Baggy shirts and sweatpants," she whispered, eyes on the floor.

Garret had to force himself to listen. Her arms came up as if to cradle herself, or maybe the baby she was remembering.

"I hid it for five months, but that night, I told him. I couldn't fight him off. I tried." She turned her head to Cora. "I tried to protect the baby, Cora. I tried so hard."

Cora nodded at her and he saw she was crying as much as Ashley.

"He left after kicking me in the stomach over and over. So many times." Ashley's whole body was wracked with shivers as she spoke. "I had the baby on the floor in the bathroom, but she didn't breathe. Didn't move. I held her and rocked her. I sang to her and wrapped her in towels. He didn't come back. I buried my baby girl and took off. Eventually, I went to Alice. Told her I was ready to leave."

"You would have needed medical care, Ash. Right?" Cora asked as if she could poke holes in this story and make it go away somehow. He almost hoped she succeeded.

Cora looked to him as if he could back her up and fix

this.

"Yes," Ashley said. "I took a bus to Austin that night, thinking I would just disappear. I grabbed a backpack and a few things and ran. But when I got to Austin, I was bleeding a lot more than I thought I would be."

Ashley didn't look at him. She talked to her sister now and he wasn't sure she remembered he was there. "There was *so much* blood, Cora. And I felt sick and weak. I thought maybe something was really wrong. So I went to the hospital."

"Did you give them your name, Ashley?" Garret needed to know as much as possible, to put as much detail into the request for a warrant as he could.

She looked at him now. "No. I gave a fake name and told them my boyfriend had gotten me pregnant and then beat me and I lost the baby. The doctor did what I expected. He called social services. When the caseworker came to see me, I gave her the same fake name and story. She left to check it and to open a file, to get the police looking for my fake boyfriend. I guess to get in touch with my parents if she could find them. While she was gone, the doctor asked me all kinds of questions and examined me. I had delivered the placenta after the baby, so there wasn't a need for a D&C. He told me the bleeding was normal and that I had to watch for fever and signs of infection."

She swiped at her cheeks with her fingertips. The tears had slowed now.

"He wanted to admit me overnight, so I said yes, but I left before the caseworker came back. Just slipped away in the chaos of the emergency room. I spent about a week sleeping in empty buildings. I looked for places with no signs of other squatters. Spots that still had some people working there during the day, like construction sites and an office building that had empty floors I could hide on. That way, I didn't run into others."

"Oh my God, Ashley," Cora said. "I can't believe you went through all of this and hid it all this time. You never told Alice what happened?" Cora seemed to be as dumbfounded as he was.

How could this have happened? How could she have gone through what she had and hidden it?

"No. After a week, I hitchhiked back to Branson Falls and went to see Alice. Bill and his wife hadn't even told her I had taken off. I refused to tell her what happened. All I would tell her was that I needed to be out of there. She had long suspected that he was..." She let the words die in her throat. "She didn't make me tell her details. I refused to testify, told her I wouldn't talk. She didn't need more than that to close the home and revoke their foster care license. She only would have needed me to talk if she was going to bring charges."

She took a deep breath. "She tried several times the first few years to get me to change my mind so she could bring charges. I knew she'd removed their license, so I didn't see any reason to talk. And I didn't want anyone to know what I had done."

"Done?" He shook his head. She hadn't *done* anything. Before he could ask anything more, she stood and he realized she'd brought the Ice Queen out again. She was protecting herself as best she could.

"Dig. You'll find all the proof you need." She walked down the hall to her room and he heard the quiet click of the door shutting behind her.

Garret sat stock still for a moment, not wanting to believe what he'd just heard. She had been *fourteen*. Fourteen when she'd been raped. When she'd gotten pregnant. When she'd been beaten so badly she lost the baby. And his head caught and stuck on one thing. *What she had done?* What had she meant by that? Because, for the life of him, he couldn't think of anything she'd *done* other than survive. Hell, that wasn't even right. She'd done so much more than simply survive.

Most kids would curl up and not come back from it, ever. Or they'd be so angry and hateful for the rest of their lives, they'd lash out. Or turn to drugs. She had not only survived, she was thriving. Sure, she'd had some setbacks the last couple of weeks. He got that. She'd had a lot of crap dredged up for her. She was dealing with memories, and—if he was right after what he'd witnessed yesterday—maybe flashbacks, too.

But if you looked at her life as a whole, she was incredible. She'd built not only one career, but two. She was a contributing member of her community, a woman people respected and looked up to. He only had to look at the large number of people who would do anything for her to know she was a good friend. It was evidenced in their commitment to her.

He raised his gaze to meet Cora's and shook his head. She looked absolutely stunned. All this time, as close as those two were, Ashley hadn't told her. He could see it in her eyes.

"I don't know if we can bring charges for what he did to Ashley. There are special rules when a minor is involved. In some cases, the statute of limitations is going to run from when the minor becomes an adult. I have to speak to the DA, see what the statute is here. But I can use this to get that child out of the home. Hopefully, with this information, the mom will take her out of the home herself, and get her away from that monster."

Cora nodded. "Do you think he killed Alice?"

He nodded. "I think it's a very good possibility. I'm going to take this to the DA. See if we can get a warrant to search the yard, dig up the baby's remains, if they're even there after all this time." He began making a mental checklist, and on top of the list was calling his friend at the state forensics lab to see if the bones from a five-month-old fetus would even be around after this length of time.

He continued aloud. "I'll try to use this to get a search warrant to see if there's anything related to Alice's murder or to Alice in the house. It's a thread to pull...finally."

Cora gestured over her shoulder. "I'm going to check on her."

He nodded and stood. As much as he wanted to go to Ashley, he couldn't. He had to follow through on what she'd just given him. He had to follow this lead and make sure the girl he'd seen was safe. And if his gut was right, Ashley needed time. She wasn't ready to see him after what she'd just revealed. He had a feeling she would need to process this. She would need to take time to get through this with her family, to come to terms with things.

"I'll let myself out," he said, then called out to Cora as she started down the hall. "Tell her I'll be back. I'm only leaving long enough to get things rolling and follow this through to get the girl out of the house. Then I'll be back." He just hoped she'd let him in when he did come back. That she wouldn't hate him. Because he was now the man who'd made her face her worst nightmare. Made her relive it.

And made her share it with the world.

ASHLEY STOOD IN BILL FRANKS' backyard and watched, flanked by her mother and Cora. She hadn't been able to stop shaking since she'd told Cora and Garret her story, and she had to fight not to turn and run from the place she'd never wanted to return to. When Garret had called to say they'd be executing the warrant and asked her if she wanted to be there, her gut reaction had been to say no. But her mother and Cora convinced her to go. They believed it would be cathartic. She wasn't sure. Images from her time here flashed through her head faster than she could process them, each bringing a fresh wave of fear and shame. She felt sick to her stomach, and the need to look over her shoulder for Bill Franks wouldn't go away, even though she knew he wasn't there.

Garret had consulted a forensics expert who felt there would be enough of the skeleton of her baby left to test for DNA. He had also talked to the DA, who said he might be willing to bring charges of manslaughter against Franks for killing the infant when he beat Ashley. It was too late to charge him for statutory rape. She didn't know what to feel about any of that yet.

Bill Franks and his girlfriend, Michelle Davis, had been taken into custody for questioning before Ashley had arrived—Franks as a suspect in Alice's murder, and Davis as a material witness. Ashley was just happy not to have to see Franks. She couldn't have handled that right now. She was barely holding it together as it was.

As she stood to the side, she watched the coroner remove the large concrete blocks that lay over the grave. A half hour later, he began to remove bones, and the empty ache she always felt when she thought of her baby came over her.

He didn't pull out the bundle of towels she'd carefully wrapped her baby in. She supposed that made sense. After ten years, they were probably nothing more than shreds at the bottom of the grave. She hadn't offered her child much in the way of a burial. The thought of the tattered material struck her hard, as if she'd left her baby exposed. She closed her eyes, not wanting to see the bones being lifted one by one and placed in a cardboard evidence box.

Forgive me.

Garret had said they would need the remains for evidence, but that she would eventually be able to claim the body and bury her daughter properly. That gave her some comfort as she stood there, heart aching with the knowledge that she had failed that little baby. Failed her in so many ways.

Please, please forgive me.

Alice had tried to get Ashley to leave the Franks' home before, always suspecting there was something going on. Ashley had refused for so many reasons, all of them complex and twisted. But one of the main reasons she hadn't was because she'd wanted to keep that baby. She hadn't wanted anyone to find out about the little girl. In her foolish, fourteen-year-old mind, she had thought she could hide the pregnancy long enough that no one could make her get rid of the baby.

And at first her stomach was only getting thick around her waist, not really sticking out the way she'd thought it would. It was only the week before the baby died that her stomach had really started protruding in any significant way.

Ashley brought her hand to her mouth and covered the sob that wanted to come out. She felt gutted, standing here watching this. Her mother's arms held her tightly, but Ashley finally turned away. From the day she'd entered their family, Mary Walker's arms had been a place of sanctuary. Right now, she couldn't have that. She couldn't stand to have anyone comforting her when there would never be comfort for the baby she'd failed.

CHAPTER SEVENTEEN

Garret waited on Ashley's front steps, wondering if she would answer the door for him. He didn't see her mother's car or Cora's, so either Ashley was out with one of them or she was here alone.

When the door opened a moment later, he had his answer.

"I wasn't sure if you'd want to see me," he said.

She didn't even look like the woman he'd known just days before. There was a wall around her a mile high right now, and everything in her body language warned him off. Told him to go away.

She wore jeans that were skintight with holes at the knees, and a loose sweatshirt with a large neckline that hung off one shoulder. She looked like a teenager, he realized. Like she was forcing herself back to when she'd lived in the Franks' home. Burying the adult Ashley and going back to the teenager who'd seen and known too much.

She tilted her head. "Why wouldn't I want to see you? Maybe you like me better now that you know what I am? Maybe you feel like you've got more of a shot to get in my pants now, Detective, huh?"

"What is it that you think you are, Ashley?" His voice was quiet, even though he wanted to grab her and shake her. He wanted her to understand that none of this was her fault. That she hadn't done anything wrong.

She shrugged. "A victim?" He knew that wasn't really her answer. That wasn't what she was thinking at all. Because she didn't see herself as a victim here. She was telling him what she thought he wanted to hear. He had a feeling her real answer was a lot less charitable toward herself.

He decided to leave it alone for now. "Can I come in?"

She didn't say anything, but stepped back, making room for him to enter.

She moved to the couch and sat, her knees pulled up to her chest, arms wrapped around them as if to hug herself. He ached to be the one doing the hugging. Holding her and letting her draw strength from him. But he didn't know what she needed from him. Didn't know how to be there for her. What to do. And her jerky movements told him to stay back.

He sat next to her on the couch, not crowding, but not going away either.

"We've arrested Bill Franks." There was no reaction. No change to her demeanor whatsoever. "Not for what he did to you. The district attorney can't arrest him for that.

The statute of limitations has run out on the statutory rape charges."

He spoke softly, but with each word, each mention of what Franks had done to her, he watched another wall go up. There were so many layers, he didn't know how he'd start to bring them down.

Her eyes shuttered, her gaze going cold and hard. He imagined the teenager who had shown up in Alice's office. Hardened. Cut off from the world. He had a feeling Ashley's adoptive parents were nothing short of miracle workers. Getting through the walls she must have had back then—the ones he saw her constructing anew right before him—must have taken very special people.

"They want to bring aggravated manslaughter charges against him for the death of your baby." Another wall went up. Her eyes were not simply hard and cold any longer. They'd gone dead. He pushed on, going on the theory that it was better to get all of this out in the open at once. Then he'd get a freaking sledgehammer if he had to, and obliterate those damned walls.

"The DA is also going to bring charges for Alice's homicide against him based on evidence we found at the home. He had a folder and notes Alice had made. Notes with your name on them, information on him from years before. It's in Alice's handwriting. We believe he took it from her apartment when he killed her. I think she was going to investigate him, that she found out he had a child in his home and was going to try to get that child out of there using testimony from you, if she could get it. I believe he stopped her before she

145

could do that. When Michelle Davis was presented with the evidence against him and the evidence of his molestation of you as a child, she stood her ground. She refuses to take her child and leave his home, even if he makes bail and comes back to the house. She doesn't believe he's a child molester. No matter what we showed her or told her, she remained convinced he'd been wrongly accused. Child Protective Services has removed the child from her care at this time."

He leaned down, forcing her eyes to meet his. "The girl is safe now, Ashley. You did that. You gave us what we needed to get her out of that house. To get her away from him. We don't think he touched her yet. She wasn't his preferred age."

A flash of...something he couldn't quite read crossed her face before she could hide it. And then he saw anger, right before she lashed out.

"I didn't protect my baby! I didn't stop him from killing my baby. Do you know how many times Alice asked me to leave that house, Garret? How many times she tried to get me to open up to her, to tell her what was going on? And do you want to know the really sick part? I tell myself I stayed so no one would find out about the baby. That I could hide it there and save up money to leave, but *I* know the truth. *I* know why I stayed. Do you want to know, too? Because maybe if you know, you'll realize what I am and you'll leave me alone. You'll get the hell out of my life."

Garret forced his body to stay at ease, his breathing to regulate. He didn't want her to see a reaction. Game face on, he responded. "Is that what you want, Ashley? For me to leave?"

Her sneer was ugly, but she didn't answer his question. "Come on, Garret. Don't detectives always want the truth? Don't you want to know why I stayed?"

She had switched to a tauntingly seductive tone. It wasn't the seductive voice he'd heard from her before—the one that was natural, that she seemed utterly unaware of as it caused an instantaneous reaction whenever he heard it. This was a falsely seductive voice he imagined her using over the years as a form of armor. As a way to keep things on her playing field, where she wanted them.

"Sure, Ashley," he said with a feigned nonchalance he didn't feel in the least. "Why don't you tell me why you stayed?"

"Because I liked it," she spat at him. She'd risen to her feet now and her whole body screamed for him to leave. Screamed, *get away*!

He didn't. He nodded. "I imagine you did."

The shock in her eyes held for a split second before she covered it with more of that false freaking bravado that chiseled away at his heart. God, she was hurting, and her pain cut into him.

Her lips curled in a snarl and he had to remind himself she was frightened. She was hurting and lashing out and protecting herself as only a fourteen-year-old girl could. Because that's what she was right now. She'd been launched back into the horrible nightmare of her existence. She'd been tossed back there and she was living it right now in front of him.

"You don't get it. I *liked* what he was doing to me. I liked that he wanted me. I liked the attention. I liked the way he made me feel. I was a whore, Garret. Nothing more than a whore. I was so happy when I got pregnant. I wanted that baby. But not for the reason you're thinking. You think I wanted something to care for. Someone to be my family. But that wasn't it. I thought if I kept the baby, if I had his baby, he'd want me forever. I thought if I gave him what his wife could never give him I could stay. I would even let her raise the baby as her own. We'd tell everyone it was their baby, and we'd all live happily ever after. That's why I wanted the baby. I was using that baby when I got her killed."

Garret kept his face blank and his gaze steady as his heart was cleaved in two by her words. By the ache in her voice. It killed him that she thought she should feel any guilt for what happened. Of course, she hadn't had the training he had in handling victims of sexual assault and molestation. His training hadn't been in depth. But he knew enough to know her feelings weren't unusual.

Victims of molestation often had mixed feelings about what was happening. It took a lot for them to realize that just because their body responded to the stimulation, it didn't make them responsible for what was done to them. And for Ashley, adding in the fact that she'd gone through life in foster care, that at fourteen she had come to realize the chances of being adopted were slim to none, you had a recipe for a kid feeling some pretty mixed-up things about her molester. It was natural that she thought the baby could bind those people to her as a family.

Garret nodded and took a step closer to her.

"I get that."

She looked thrown. Confused. She opened her mouth as though she wanted to keep arguing, to keep pushing him away, but he didn't let her. He ran his hands down the backs of her arms and tugged her to him when his fingers hit hers. "I get it, Ashley. I get it and I still think you're a good person. I still think it wasn't your fault. I still think you didn't kill your baby. You're not responsible for that. You couldn't protect your baby any more than you could protect yourself back then."

"No." She shook her head almost as violently as her hands were trembling. "No...I...you don't understand. He didn't discover the pregnancy that night. It wasn't like I gained enough weight to show and he discovered it. He was too drunk most of the time to know. I *told* him. I waited for him to come to me that night and I told him. I—"

He didn't let her finish. He finished for her. "*You*, Ashley, are a good person. *You* are a beautiful, strong, incredible person. Nothing that was done to you back then, and none of the choices and decisions you made as a result, can change that. You're a good person."

He could see the slight sheen of tears threatening to fall, but she shook her head again, as though she could will them back. But he was also starting to see the veneer crack. He could see the adult Ashley pushing her way through. The

149

one who knew in her head and her heart that she couldn't be blamed for what happened all that time ago. For what happened to her when she was really no more than a child.

"Don't do this," she whispered, the plea in her voice bringing the anguish in his heart to a full boil. But he wouldn't walk away from her now. She needed to hear this, needed to face it.

He squeezed her hands in his and kept going, knocking down the final wall she'd been clinging to. "I get it. You think it would be easier if I hated you. If I walked away. Because that would be less scary than this. I get that. But nothing you say, nothing you tell me, will make me hate you. What he did to you had nothing to do with you. It was *him*, Ashley. All him. *He* raped you. *He* killed your baby. The fact that you liked the attention, even wanted some of it to continue—the fact that you stayed—doesn't change that. It doesn't put any of it on you."

Her body went beyond trembling. She was shaking violently now, as though a battle was going on inside her. But it was a battle against herself. Something had to die inside of her to end the battle. He only hoped it was the guilt that fourteen-year-old girl was carrying around. Not the Ashley he knew. Not the Ashley he wanted to know better.

CHAPTER EIGHTEEN

shley cried for what seemed like hours, her throat aching, her chest heaving in uncontrollable bursts. Garrett had brought her to the couch and sat with her, holding her in his strong arms the entire time. He didn't seem to care that her nose was running all over his shirt. When her jagged breaths slowed, she waited for him to say something, but he didn't. He seemed to have no judgment. He simply held her. Just as she had held her baby so many years earlier.

"I held her for hours. He left the house and Tanya hadn't come home that night. I sat on the floor of the bathroom and held my baby for hours. She was so tiny. She fit right in my hands and weighed nothing, Garret, nothing." She cupped her hands together and looked at them. She had never been able to get rid of the sensation of holding that tiny weightless baby in her hands. It would sneak up on her at times, along with the doubts, the gnawing fear that she would never be a good enough person after what she'd done.

"I won't ever be good enough."

"Good enough for what?" His voice was gruff, but calm.

Ashley frowned. "I don't know. Even though I love my family and I know they love me, I think I've always had this feeling that I don't deserve them."

Garret was quiet and Ashley didn't speak again for a long time, either. When she did, her voice shook. "If I had told Alice what happened back then, she wouldn't be dead now."

Garret pulled back and turned her to face him, hands on her shoulders. "No, Ashley. You can't blame yourself for the decisions you made as a fourteen-year-old put in a horrific situation. Hell, I'll get you the science if you need it, on the underdeveloped mind of a teen and the inability of a child that age to make these kinds of decisions. But believe me, you are not responsible for this. Bill Franks is responsible for his actions. He's responsible for what he did to you, for what he did to your baby, and for what he did to Alice. Him. No one else."

Ashley nodded, but didn't say anything. She didn't know if she could let go of the feelings of guilt so easily. Her head said to believe what Garret was telling her, but her heart said otherwise. And now she had a new measure of guilt to stack on top of the rest. Because she knew Garret wanted more than simply a witness for his case or even a friend. She wasn't an idiot. His interest in something more came through loud and clear.

Her body was interested in that, too. But her head was so screwed up she didn't know if she could offer him anything. She sure as hell didn't know how to explain that, although she'd used sex to seek out intimacy with boys when she was a teen, she'd realized at some point that wasn't going to get her what she wanted. It wouldn't get her a real relationship with a man. Sex wasn't the answer for her as a teen any more than it had been the way to find a family who loved her when she lived in the Franks' house. Sex created illusions of relationships, but underneath, there were only smoke and mirrors.

And when Ashley had realized that, she'd stopped using sex for anything at all. How could she tell Garret it had been almost eight years since she'd been naked with someone of the opposite sex? She dreamed about the fantasy of a loving, intimate relationship with a man like Garret. In fact, she'd built a writing career based on those fantasies, that illusive dream. But that didn't mean she ever thought she was capable of attaining that. She'd never once come close to having the sort of relationships she wrote about. In fact, she might as well be writing science fiction. Her stories were as fantastical to her as a trip to Mars or a time-traveling doctor.

As if reading the truth on her face, Garrett kissed her temple and pulled her into his arms for a hug. He was letting her off the hook, she realized. Part of her was relieved. But underneath, a small part of her felt the loss of what could be with this man. If only she could be brave enough to go for it. The only trouble was, Ashley wasn't feeling up to any more bravery right now. She wanted to hide and lick her wounds and figure out how to move forward in her life from here.

"I'm going to get you a better lawyer," Michelle said into the phone, looking into the eyes of the man she loved. A man she knew could never do the things they said he'd done. She knew for a fact he hadn't done what they thought he had.

"Oh yeah," Bill said, eyes flat. "How you plan to do that, little miss thing? You got money I don't know about somewhere? Because lawyers cost money."

Michelle put her hand to the glass, but Bill didn't raise his in response. His gaze looked through her, as if she was useless to him. But she wasn't. She would show him.

She raised her chin. "I don't know how I'll do it, but I'll find a way to pay for one for you. Those public defenders are useless, you know. But I'll take care of things for you, Bill. I'll find a way."

His eyes swung to her now, but that familiar hardness she'd seen in him from time to time was there. The hardness he got when he was angry. When she'd done something wrong. "You know what you can do for me, Chelle?"

He used her pet name, but it wasn't said with any tenderness, and she swallowed hard. She reminded herself he was going through something extremely difficult right now. He wouldn't ever admit it to her, but she knew he had to be scared. She'd always heard child molesters didn't do well in prison, and the split lip and bandage across his nose told her he wasn't faring well in there. The injustice of it ate at her. To be falsely accused of something so horrific was awful.

They were railroading him. The damned social workers who had come to take Evie didn't want to listen to a word she said. She told them over and over he wasn't interested in kids. He'd never so much as peeked at Evie. Hell, just before they'd come to the house with that fucking warrant, Michelle had been bent over the kitchen table lifting her skirt for him. He wanted *her,* not a damned kid.

"Anything, Billy. Tell me what to do."

He looked around and then turned back to her, cradling the phone tight to his ear. He bent toward the glass and lowered his voice. "If that girl wasn't around, I wouldn't be in this mess. It's *her*. It's all *her*."

Michelle didn't understand. What girl? He couldn't mean Evie. "Who?"

He mumbled something about not leaving loose ends years ago. Then he tapped the phone receiver against the glass before lifting it back to his ear again. "You take care of that Walker girl, you hear me? You want to help me? That's the way to do it. She needs to disappear, you hear me? Huh?"

She sat motionless for a minute, before looking around nervously. "I—I don't know, Billy."

He slammed the receiver back into its cradle, drawing the two guards at either end of the room forward. He pointed at the glass and said something, but the words were lost behind the thick separation.

She called out to him not to go, but the guards had stepped forward, speaking words she couldn't hear. Clearly demands, from the looks of it. Billy turned with a glare her way before walking toward a door, flanked by officers.

"I'll take care of it, Billy," she called through the glass, garnering a glare from the uniformed guard on her side of the partition. She ducked her head and tucked her purse in against her side, hugging it with one arm as she walked toward the door. She'd figure something out. She didn't know what, but Billy was counting on her and she wasn't about to let him down.

CHAPTER NINETEEN

Two days after what Ashley now thought of as "the big breakdown," Garret knocked on her door with a tiny bouquet in his hands. Not a giant bouquet of dozens of roses you sometimes read about in billionaire romance novels. Not even a grocery-store bouquet of carnations and lilies. It was a little posy of what looked like peonies and wildflowers, and even some branches and leaves. And it was somehow better than anything Ashley could have come up with herself.

He smiled and passed it over to her. "For you."

Ashley suddenly didn't feel the embarrassment she was sure she'd feel when seeing him for the first time after her meltdown. She took the flowers and smiled as she led him to the kitchen.

"Thank you. Did you pick them yourself?" She smoth-ered a laugh as she pulled out a small glass jar and placed the flowers in it before filling it with water from the tap. "They're beautiful."

"Thanks. And yes, I did." He sounded smug, like he'd accomplished some great feat. It made her giggle. "Are you laughing at me, Ashley Walker?"

She grinned at him. "Sorry. It's just the image of you picking flowers is a little—" She stopped to think before continuing. "Incongruent."

Now he laughed. "Yeah, well, maybe it wasn't all me. I live in an apartment next to this little house with the sweetest lady next door. She's about eighty-one or eighty-two now, I think. But she's out gardening every day. I stopped to talk to her and mentioned I was going to get you some flowers. I asked her what I should get you and she made me come in her garden with her and pick them. The leaves were all me, though," he said, pointing to the branches that stuck out between the peonies. "I thought it added a touch of manliness to the whole thing."

His smile was teasing and she laughed at the look on his face. He was really and truly proud of his manly bouquet. And she had to admit, she was a little bit, too. It showed he cared about what he gave her. That he wanted to bring her something pretty, something that would put a smile on her face. It ended up doing more than that. Her heart jumped a little bit and she began to feel hopeful that maybe, just maybe, she could open up to this man. Let her guard down enough to let him inside and see what happened.

Garret smiled at the glass jar and tapped it with his finger. "Alice did that, too. Used glass jars for flowers and chipped coffee mugs to hold her pennies on the kitchen table."

Ashley looked at him. "You knew Alice?"

He nodded, his eyes sad. "Yeah." He ran a hand over his jaw and gave her a look. "Listen, my captain doesn't know. I need you to keep that to yourself so I can stay on this case."

Now it was Ashley's turn to nod. "How did you know her?"

He pulled out a stool and sat at the kitchen island, then watched as Ashley did the same. She watched him, but didn't seem to be judging him. He hoped like hell he was doing the right thing by telling her this.

"I grew up in the apartment down the hall from her." He stopped and waited, but she didn't say anything. "My mom tried really hard. She wasn't going to win any medals for mom of the year, but she really tried. I had clothes, food, a few toys and things. I had what I needed. And she loved me. She just wasn't around a lot."

Garret felt like an ass, saying anything critical about his upbringing after what Ashley had been through, but he plugged on. "My mom had no education. She dropped out of high school to have me, and honestly, before that I think she failed just about everything. She just wasn't interested in learning. But then she had me and she needed to work two or three minimum-wage jobs at a time to take care of us. To make sure we lived in a place where I was safe. It wasn't the best neighborhood, but it wasn't the worst."

Ashley smiled at him. "It sounds like she loved you."

He felt himself smiling at the memory of his mom. "She

did in her own way. She just, hell, I don't know how to describe it. She was just tired, I think. I mean, yeah, she was tired from working three jobs, but I think she was also very tired of life in general. Her parents disowned her when she had me. My dad took off well before I was born. I still don't know much about him other than I have his name, and I guess it doesn't matter. He obviously had no interest in me. I think my mom was just pretty tired of the whole world. Of the way things had gone for her."

"Where is she now?" Ashley asked.

"She died when I was nineteen. She had a heart attack." He could still hear the shock in his own voice. "At thirty-five, after working herself to the bone all my life, hell, all her life. She just died one day. Her heart just stopped."

Garret looked down and found his hands in Ashley's, her thumbs rubbing circles over his fingers. "I'm so sorry, Garret."

He nodded. "It's still a shock all this time later."

He paused for a long time, just thinking about his mom. She had been a good woman. She just hadn't been the one to teach him that it was okay to reach for things in life. To teach him to want more out of life.

"Alice was there for me through it, just like she'd been there for me all my life." His voice was gruff now with the memories. Memories of two women who had meant the world to him, but were now gone. "She always brought me a little snack for after dinner. Or she'd have me over for lemonade and ask me about my day. My mom and I didn't have those talks. If she wasn't working, she was sleeping.

She'd leave me dinner on a plate in the oven or money to buy pizza. Alice was the one who would make me eat a piece of fruit or a vegetable here or there. Like she was supplementing my upbringing."

Ashley laughed. "That sounds like Alice. She couldn't ignore anyone that needed her. If she thought she could help, she would. And if she didn't think she could help, she'd find someone who could."

Garret smiled at her and squeezed her hands. "I wouldn't be a cop if not for Alice. She was the one who taught me I could reach for more than my mom had. She taught me to look at the world and see what was out there that I could strive for. My mom never did that. Not for me and not for herself. She just wanted to get by. I don't think it ever occurred to her to want more. But Alice always told me I could be whatever I wanted to be."

They sat for a long time talking about their memories of Alice. Ashley told him how Alice had been her only caseworker, which wasn't always the case for kids in the system. Kids often got shuffled around, or caseworkers burned out and moved on. Not Alice. Once you were hers, you were hers for life, if she had anything to say about it.

Ashley had met her soon after her mom had left her at a playground when she was seven. Even at the young age of seven, she had been angry and defensive, telling the world— and Alice—she didn't need anyone to take care of her. "I got this," she used to say. "I got this." Like she was old enough to see to her own needs. And Alice had smiled and told her she'd just help out then. Give a little support here and there when Ashley needed it.

Ashley and Garret moved through the week in much the same way, telling each other stories. The stories that defined them. She learned a little more about his parents. His father had come over as a teenager on his own from Ireland. When he and Garret's mother met, they thought it was very *Romeo and Juliet* of them to date, given his Irish roots and her British heritage, even though his mother had never set foot in England. In fact, she'd never set foot outside of Texas. His dad stuck around long enough to get his mom pregnant, before leaving her alone and heartbroken.

Ashley didn't have even a scrap of information on her biological father. Her mother had been too wasted to talk to her about much, right up until the moment she abandoned her. She used to fantasize that he would show up and take her away. Take her home after explaining the huge mix-up at the hospital when she was born or that he'd been lost at sea and couldn't get back to her. Little wonder she ended up as a writer years later. She'd been weaving stories for a long time.

Ashley smiled at Garret as they left her parents' house a week later. He'd taken her to dinner twice that week, but hadn't pushed for anything more than a kiss goodnight at her door. Somehow, though, his kisses started a burning inside she hadn't expected from such slight contact of his mouth on hers.

She didn't know if it was the way his mouth was both

soft and firm at the same time. Or the way his body pressed toward her ever so slightly, hovering just enough to let her feel the warmth, the promise of more. Or the way his hands came up to cup her cheeks. Or all of it. She sighed. It was probably all of it.

Garret took her hand in his as they walked down the drive to his car. "Is it always that—"

"Crazy? Insane? Chaotic?"

"Yeah. That."

She laughed and let him tug her close when they reached the passenger side of his car. He held both of her hands in his, but wrapped her arms around his back before putting his arms around her. She felt safe, but the anticipation of what was to come sent a whirlwind of butterflies dancing through her. No, not butterflies. An entire hive of honeybees, all buzzing crazily in her stomach.

Her hands brushed up his black polo shirt and she felt a corresponding tingle of awareness rush through her.

"I had a really good time today," he said, with that little bit of gruffness to his voice that sent shivers through her. The kind of voice she wrote about that said her hero had something on his mind that should probably be happening behind closed doors.

"I did, too," she said, and she meant it. They'd gone for a hike that afternoon before going to her family's Sunday dinner, which was anything but routine. Ashley had never laughed as hard as she had when she'd watched Cora and Emma grill Garret about his "intentions" toward their sister. The boys hadn't even had to lift a finger to defend her honor. Her mama bear sisters had taken that role on wholeheartedly.

Watching Garret squirm had been entirely too entertaining. But then her heart had damned near flip-flopped out of her chest and onto the floor when he had looked Ashley right smack in the eye as he'd answered them. "I plan to do everything I can to get her to fall for me. To convince her I'm good enough for her. To see that one day she'll want everything I'm willing to give her and more," he had said.

Well, thunk. She gave up the fight. There was her damned heart right on the floor.

And now he held her as though she might break. Firm enough for her to feel safe and wanted in his arms, but gentle enough, she knew he'd never use all the strength he possessed against her.

"It's going to take everything I have in me to drop you off on your front porch again tonight," he said as he nuzzled her neck, brushing his lips to the skin just below her ear.

Part of her wanted to tell him he shouldn't fight it, he should take her inside instead of leaving her on the porch, but another part knew that would be a mistake. She needed to get to the point where she felt comfortable telling him anything, talking to him about all that needed to be said. If she couldn't do that, she had no business having him in her bed yet. *She* knew that. It was her body that was having trouble with the concept. She leaned her head to the side and he nipped at her neck.

She might have moaned. Yeah, she had. All needy and wanton like the romance novelist she was. Damn.

"But, I will," he said, pulling back.

Will what?

He must have seen from the look on her face she had no clue what he was talking about. His laugh was easy and genuine and it warmed her all over again. "I *will* leave you on the porch, Ashley," he explained. "Until you're ready for more. Then I'll take you inside and make love to you all night."

He punctuated his promise with those tantalizing lips of his, kissing her senseless. She was both relieved and disappointed. Disappointed in herself that she wasn't ready yet, but relieved that he knew it and wasn't going to push her.

But oh, her body. Her body seemed to be on board with the make-love-all-night option.

"Hey, hey, hey, you two!"

Crap. Her brother, Sam, stood on the front porch, his car keys in hand, one arm covering his eyes as though tragically wounded. "Take it home where we can't see it, at least."

Ashley bit her lip. "Sorry," she whispered into Garret's dancing eyes.

He reached behind her and opened the car door, tucking her into the seat before waving to her brother. "Night, Sam."

"Yeah, yeah. Stop mauling my sister in public. In fact, stop mauling her altogether."

165

Ashley watched as Garret laughed and jogged around the front of the car.

He kept his promise, kissing her goodnight on the porch before sending her mushy brain and distinctly turned-on body inside to bed. Alone.

MICHELLE PACED THE LIVING ROOM, looking around at the mess the police had left when they'd searched the house. Fucking bullies, that's what they were. They bullied their way in with that warrant full of lies, then claimed Billy did all kinds of unspeakable things. Then they helped those damned social workers bully her daughter away from her. As if she hadn't always taken good care of Evie.

Someone from social services had called to arrange a supervised visit with Evie. *Ha!* As if her daughter needed to be protected from her. She told them she'd see her daughter when they were ready to let her see her alone. Not a minute before. She wasn't about to let those fucking busybody bullies from child services push her around. She'd watched her own mom be pushed around by them for years. She and her sisters and brothers would be taken away and her mom would practically fawn over the caseworkers trying to get them back. *They need to be with their mommy,* she would say.

Her "mommy" had never been able to put enough food on the damned table for all of them. She wasn't capable of taking care of all of them. Not like Michelle. Michelle knew how to take care of her own. She wouldn't kiss ass and kowtow to get Evie back. They could damn well hold on to her until she became such a nuisance to them—they'd come begging to Michelle to take her off their hands. Begging to have her let off the state's dime. That kid was always underfoot. The foster parents would be calling the social workers soon asking when they'd let her go home.

In the meantime, Michelle needed to figure out how to take care of Bill. *He* needed her right now. And she'd be there for him. If she was there for him now—if she proved herself—he'd never let her go. He'd want to marry her. He'd love her forever.

"It's just a matter of courage, really," she said to herself, hands fisted at her sides. She had done it before and she would do it again. That was all. It was a simple matter of courage.

She sat on the couch and looked around at the mess, not sure where to begin to clean up. She was unsure of a lot of things. The biggest of all was where to find the courage to do what Bill needed her to do. Michelle put her head in her hands and closed her eyes. For now, she would wait. Maybe his lawyer would come up with something. She had to hope whoever was assigned to represent him would know what to do, so she wouldn't have to act. Because she didn't know how she could stomach what needed to be done.

CHAPTER TWENTY

Ashley and Garret had taken to sitting on the porch swing after dinner most nights. On the nights Garret could get away from work, that is. His schedule was more demanding than Ashley's, and he never knew from one night to the next if he'd be called in for a case, but when he could join her for dinner, he did. Then there was the issue of distance. It was an hour and a half from Branson Falls to Evers.

He'd often drive the distance to pick her up, then take her outside of town for dinner, given Evers's limited selection of restaurants, before driving her home. She worried about that, knowing he had to work early most days, but he told her he was used to functioning on little sleep.

Ashley leaned into his shoulder, loving the comfort of his arms around her and his chin resting on her head. She knew she needed to come clean with him. They'd been getting closer and closer to sleeping together, and God, she wanted to. She really did. She just didn't know what he would think of her when he realized her experience was limited to her teen years. She didn't have any experience being in a healthy sexual relationship with a grown man.

"Garret?"

"Yeah?"

"I need to tell you some things," she began.

"Anything," he said, using his foot to kick-start the swing again, continuing their lazy back and forth. The easiness in his tone belied the thickening tension swirling in the air around them.

Ashley had never been one to hold back, so she took a deep breath and blurted it all out. "I haven't slept with anyone since I was seventeen."

She felt the slight freezing of his limbs before he loosened them. He didn't answer so she kept going. "What happened with Bill Franks...I guess for some people, it would have made sex seem unappealing, even frightening. Something to be avoided at all costs. But it didn't for me. I didn't enjoy it exactly, but I wasn't as scarred from it as one might think I would be. Well, not scarred in the way you would expect, anyway. Instead of trying to avoid ever being in that position again, I saw it as something I could use."

His murmured response encouraged her to go on. "I used sex to try to manipulate guys, to try to create closeness where there really wasn't any. To try to make myself feel like I belonged, like I was wanted. You name it, I used sex for it. Oral sex was something I used a lot, because, well, I guess because on some level I didn't really want to have intercourse all that much. I mean, I did, but more often than not I would try to get away with other things."

"That changed?" he asked.

"Yeah." She nodded, even though he wasn't looking at her. He kept his gaze straight ahead and she sensed he was trying to make this easier on her. She wasn't at all proud of the way she'd been when she was younger. She'd been lucky. The Walkers had loved her and adopted her when she thought she'd never have a prayer of finding that kind of acceptance. That kind of love. And yet she'd put them through hell those first few years. Sneaking out, fighting with her adopted siblings, and being known as the town slut. Not exactly something she was proud of. It had taken a lot to overcome it, especially in a town this size.

"It was Sam who helped me figure out that what I was doing wouldn't lead anywhere good. I don't know if he even meant to. He just looked at me one day when the rumors about me giving Paul Cantor a blow job behind the bleachers were all around school, even though that was actually one time I hadn't done what people said I did. Sam just looked at me and asked how that was working out for me? You know, kind of in this snotty way only a big brother could, but something about it struck me. I think it was the bit of sadness in his eyes. He sounded like a snotty older brother, but he didn't look like one.

"He looked at me like he was sad for me. Not disappointed, not disgusted. Truly sad. And suddenly, I was sad for myself. It struck me that what I was doing wasn't getting me anywhere. I wasn't finding the intimacy I wanted so badly. Because sex didn't equal intimacy. I wasn't going to get close to these guys by doing what I was doing, by giving them what I was. I was only going to hurt myself in the long run. So I stopped."

He pulled her even closer, holding her tightly to him as she continued.

"The talk didn't stop right away. If anyone wanted to brag about how great they were, how cool they were, they talked about banging Ashley Walker. It took a long time and there are people in town who won't ever forget, but eventually a lot of people realized I wasn't sneaking away at parties anymore. I was sticking with groups of other girls. I was hanging out around my brothers more. I was sticking where people could see that I wasn't off in the back of a car with a guy somewhere. Eventually, I started to like myself more. I began to care about who I was. I think I started to value myself. I started to see what my family and friends saw in me, and I don't know," she shrugged one shoulder, "I just seemed to get it. I just realized what I was doing wasn't going to get me what I wanted. And it wasn't going to make me feel better about myself. I had to do that all on my own."

She paused for a minute, feeling like she'd lifted an elephant from her chest, but still wondering what he was thinking. "Anyway, I just never really found someone I wanted to be with after that. Not enough to go through this conversation, I guess."

He cleared his throat. "Good. So...no pressure then, huh?"

Ashley burst out laughing as he grinned at her, and the

tension she'd felt was gone. But then his gaze dropped to her mouth and she saw the heat in his eyes, saw what he wanted. In an instant, the tension she'd felt moments before took on a new form. Her body warmed and she felt her breath catch simply from the look in his eyes.

He leaned in, his mouth hovering over hers, separated only by the barest of breaths. "Invite me in, Ashley."

It was part plea and part command. All sexy and all male. And all she needed. She nodded, and instantly he pulled her up, taking her hand in his and walking through her front door by her side.

Ashley had spent the last couple of years writing scenes filled with sexual tension, sensual passion, and heat meant to burn up the pages of her books. A small part of her had been half afraid when she finally did take a man to bed, it would be a letdown compared to the fantasy world she lived in. Garret proved her wrong within seconds of closing the door and turning the deadbolt lock.

He lowered his mouth to her shoulder and grazed her skin with his teeth. "Are you sure you're ready for this, Ashley?" His words were husky and low, the heat of his breath another caress across her bare skin. He'd done it on purpose, she knew. And she loved it. Reveled in it as every part of her body began a low hum of appreciation, anticipation, and arousal.

She arched into him, her breasts brushing the hard contours of his chest as he groaned. "Yes. I'm absolutely one hundred percent completely sure." She didn't want there to be any doubt.

His laugh was husky and devolved into another groan as her mouth found the hot skin in the vee where his shirt unbuttoned.

Her hands shook as she moved them up to his shoulders, where she gripped him hard, pulling him to her. She wanted more of him, more contact, more heat, more—everything. She felt his arms come around her and lift her, holding her body pressed tightly to his as he walked them back to her bedroom. And then he was laying her back, coming down on top of her as his hands and mouth continued to explore her body.

This was nothing like the awkward coming together of bodies she'd experienced as a teen. This was passion. Mutual passion where each of them wanted nothing more than to bring pleasure to the other.

He held his weight off of her as he stripped her of her clothes, then pulled his own shirt off. He kept his jeans on, the hard length of his erection evident just the same. Ashley wriggled, wanting him inside her, but wanting other things as well. She wanted to taste him and have him taste her. She wanted to feel every inch of him. His skin was so soft, yet beneath it, taut muscles rippled and tempted her at every turn. As she touched him, her body began to swell with an aching need for him. The kind of need that had her hips pulsing as he took her nipple between his teeth and teased it to life.

As she tried to hold onto her sanity, his hand slipped between her legs, spreading the moisture he found there over her clitoris. Once, twice, again and again as she began to writhe and moan in his arms. And still, it wasn't enough.

"Please," she whispered. "I need more, Garret. More of you."

She clutched at his jeans, wrenching the button free and reaching her hand in to his cock, hard and ready. She wanted to feel it stretching her, impaling her. Pounding into her over and over. At her urging, he shucked his jeans and found a condom, but before she could wrap her legs around his waist and trap him against her, he was gone. She felt momentarily self-conscious when he drew one leg over his shoulder as his mouth came down on her, but then he was suckling, licking, nipping—and she was lost.

He spun her up to the heavens and back down again, drawing an orgasm from her so intense, she thought she might have blacked out for a moment. Without letting her recover, he was there, inside of her, right where she'd needed him all along. Pressing into her hard and deep, and God, it felt so incredible, she could only gasp and hold tightly to him.

"Ashley." The word was ground out between his clenched jaws, and she knew his need was as great as hers. She reached between their bodies and grasped the shaft of his penis as he pulled from her, letting her hand work him as he plunged in and out of her. He slowed to let her tease and taunt, sweat beading on his brow.

"You're killing me, Ashley."

"Should I stop?" she whispered as she watched him sink back into her.

"Never."

But then he gave her no choice but to stop as he cupped her behind and lifted her hips, increasing the pace, the depth, as he sank into her over and over. She couldn't do anything more than hang on, struggling to meet his thrusts with her own. And as she felt him come, her body clenched, her muscles gripping him tightly in ecstasy. Sheer pleasure tore through her in wave after wave. And she knew she didn't want to give this man up. Ever.

"You NEED to get me out of here, Chelle." Michelle's heart broke seeing Bill so beaten down. His face now sported black and blue marks in various stages of healing, and his nose looked like it had suffered repeated blows. There was an edge of desperation to his voice she'd never heard before.

"I—I'm working on it, Bill. I just have to figure out how." She had spent the morning following that damned librarian, watching her go to the grocery store, living it up at a coffee shop with friends, and then meeting that fucking pig cop who had put Bill here. The woman was a whore. That much was clear. She'd tried to trap Bill into some kind of sick relationship when she was young and now she was fucking the cop on the case to try and screw Bill over. All while she waltzed around free and clear.

But Michelle was still trying to figure out how to do what Bill had told her needed to be done. She needed to get up the courage to do it—and she was—but she also needed to come up with a plan. She couldn't just walk up to the woman and do it right in the open. She needed time to figure things out. She looked down at the nail she had chewed to the quick, before glancing nervously back up at Bill.

His eyes turned hard and cold and he leaned into the glass, his knuckles white where they clenched the receiver. "You said you'd take care of it, Michelle. You told me I could count on you."

She nodded. "I know. I'll do it. It's taken care of, I swear. It's all taken care of."

In a heartbeat, he flipped a switch and was back to begging. She'd never seen him beg like this. It troubled her.

"Please, baby. Please, you gotta do something. I can't stay in here. I can't be here."

She raised her hand to the glass. "I'll handle it, Billy. I'll handle her."

CHAPTER TWENTY-ONE

Ashley rolled over in her bed and reached for the source of heat beside her. She smiled when her hands found Garret's chest and he rolled toward her almost instantly. She smiled wider when her hands moved down his body to find him hard and ready for her. Her body was just as eager as his. Soft and ready to take him into her.

He had spent the night at her house almost every night that week, even when he didn't wrap up work until late. She wasn't nuts about him making the long drive when he was tired after a long day, but he didn't want her on the road alone at night. It was sweet, if a little alpha. But she could handle alpha. Well, a little bit of alpha, anyway.

He rolled her under him and began to lace her body with those maddening kisses of his. She pressed against him, knowing they didn't have much time, but wanting to spend hours anyway. When his hand found her wet and swollen between her legs, he grinned. "Dreaming of me, gorgeous?"

"Uh-uh. Johnny Depp," she deadpanned, earning a growl and a swat to her backside.

She moaned and wriggled in his arms. "Again," she whispered, drawing an answering moan from him as he smacked her again, before kneading the spot with his hand. The response from her body was instantaneous and heady.

"God, what you do to me, Ashley," he said after he'd donned a condom and lined himself up at her entrance. He didn't keep her waiting long, plunging into her depths, and bringing them both to climax more quickly than she thought possible.

As he held her afterward, she slowly kissed her way up his chest, to the strong shoulders she was becoming accustomed to leaning on. She nibbled with her teeth, as he slid one large hand up and down her side. *This*, she could get used to. The waking up together.

And the going to bed together, for that matter.

And the in between, as a matter of fact, she thought as she remembered the way he'd taken her slowly, sleepily, in the middle of the night. Yes, she could get used to all of it.

"Shower?" he asked.

She raised her head and eyed the clock. "Ugh. A fast one. You'll have to stay on your side of the line, mister. I have to be at work in less than forty minutes."

"There's a line now? First Johnny Depp, now a line." His smile was wide as he stood and pulled her from the bed, leading her to the bathroom.

He didn't stay on his side of the line at all, but he did manage to get her out the door with two minutes to spare.

Her hair was wet and she was wearing two different socks, but she had a smile on her face.

That smile stayed in place for the rest of the day. Her first few days back at the library after word had gotten around about her past had been hard. The kids had been awkward with her, not able to look her in the eye. Some of the adults who came in had looked at her as though something were wrong with her, and she had gone back to feeling like somehow it was her fault. Like she'd been the one to do something wrong, not Bill Franks. She had a feeling those emotions would stay with her always, never fully going away.

Then Haddie had walked into the library, marched up to Ashley, and pulled her into a tight hug. She'd held her a long time, then pulled back and said, "You're a strong, strong girl to have gone through that and still be such an important, loving part of our community now." She'd said it loudly, then turned to look at the other people in the library, before turning to Ashley again. "A strong girl and an incredible woman. I'm so proud to know you."

And with that, she had walked away as though nothing had happened. Old John Holland had shown up next. He'd walked in, grabbed the morning paper he always came to read, stopped at the circulation desk, and put his hand on hers. He had simply squeezed her hand, then patted it a few times. With a grunt, he was off to his table in the corner by the window to read.

And that seemed to be that. People went on about their business then, as though nothing had changed. And Ashley had to be honest, she'd never been so grateful in her life. Those two had seemingly made an announcement to the town. She would not be ostracized or cast out or made to feel dirty for what had happened. She would simply continue to be Ashley. Their librarian and writer of smut under a fake name.

And so, a week later, she left the library with her smile still firmly intact. She wouldn't be seeing Garret tonight, but that was all right. He was attending a bachelor party for one of the animal control officers in his town. He had tried to tell her he could drive to her house after the party broke up, but she didn't want him making the drive late at night after drinking. He, of course, countered that he didn't need to drink, but she told him no.

It wasn't that she didn't love seeing him every night. But Ashley played the love expert card given her status as a romance novelist and told him it was important for them to have alone time, as well as together time. She had a hot bath with a glass of wine in mind. After that, she planned to paint her toenails and maybe sit down and see if she could add a few thousand words to her work-in-progress. She'd just begun the first book in a new series, and she was eager to have a little quiet time to get some of it down on paper.

Ashley had always found if she didn't write fast enough for her characters, they never shut up in her head. So long as she got enough down on paper in a given week, she'd keep the voices at bay. Not *those* kind of voices. No one was telling her to do things in the name of Satan or anything like that. They just jibber-jabbered in there, sketching scenes and staging plotlines day in and day out. It could wear a girl out if she wasn't careful.

She locked the library doors after one final scan of the room to be sure all the lights were out and the copy machines shut down for the night. On the short walk home, she texted Garret. *Don't do anything I wouldn't do.*

It took only a minute to get his message back. *I'm rolling my eyes at you. Good to know my options are wide open for the night.*

Ha! I think I should be offended, she typed back.

Sure you don't want me to drive there? I can stop drinking now.

No, she typed back and then typed in a smiley face. *I plan to write and take a bubble bath.*

Shit. A bubble bath without me? That's just cruel.

LOL. We'll take one tomorrow night. Promise.

Damn. Now I have a hard-on in the middle of the party. Nice, Ash. Real nice.

Happy to be of service.

Service. Christ, woman. You're killing me.

LOL Night!

Ugh. Night.

Ashley laughed and tucked her phone back in her pocket. She couldn't help picturing them in a tub full of bubbles together. Damn. Maybe she should tell him to make the drive tonight.

It wasn't until she was practically on top of her driveway that she realized there was a car in front of the house and a woman standing by the passenger door, all but wringing her hands. The woman looked distraught, and Ashley's heart automatically went out to her, even though she had no idea who she was or what could be wrong.

The woman stepped forward. "Ashley? Ashley Walker? Could I, um, could I talk to you?"

And then it hit Ashley. Could this woman be another of Bill Franks' victims? Garret had said they might need her to testify about what had happened to her as part of proving Franks' motive for killing Alice. The theory was that Alice had discovered he had a child in his house and he had killed her when she confronted him and wouldn't back off.

The only thing they were stuck on so far was how Bill Franks got into Alice's house. There had been no sign he'd forced his way in. It looked like her killer had been invited into her home, and Ashley and Garret both knew Alice wouldn't have done that. But who knew, maybe he'd had a gun or something.

Ashley walked over to the woman and offered a reluctant smile. The thought of talking with another of Franks' victims made her stomach churn. She didn't want to relive that time in her life for anything, but she felt a wave of guilt. Maybe this woman needed someone to talk to. Maybe she needed help. Or maybe she wanted to come forward and help in building a case against Franks. At the very least, Ashley could give her Garret's information.

"Yes, I'm Ashley Walker," she said, stepping close to the other woman. It was in that split second that several things happened at once. Although they happened in what seemed to be slow motion, Ashley couldn't move quickly enough to do anything, to react in any way.

First, she wondered how the woman knew her name. She wasn't one hundred percent sure if her name had been included in the warrant for Bill Franks' house or not, but even if it had been, where would this woman have gotten that information? Unless maybe this woman had been contacted by Garret or his partner and then had just asked in Evers for Ashley? It was a small town where she was well known, after all. She dismissed the idea. Surely they wouldn't have given out Ashley's name.

In the seconds her mind grappled with this puzzle, she felt a tingling awareness crawl up her spine. Something wasn't right. And that's when the second thing happened. She saw a sneer cross the woman's face as Ashley came close. The faintest hint that the woman wasn't a friend after all. That she wasn't someone who wanted comfort or reassurance or friendship from Ashley.

And it was then that Ashley saw the woman's hand slip from her pocket with something large and black in it. In slow motion she watched the woman raise the object and then her body went rigid as a pain she'd never imagined raced through her. She couldn't move. It felt like she couldn't breathe, only she must have because she didn't pass out. She thought she might be screaming, but wasn't sure anything was coming out.

With no one to hold her up, her body fell, her head slamming into the grass, hitting the hard ground beneath it with a thud. The pain racing on an electric current through her body was unbearable. She tried to force her limbs to move, but there was no way it was happening. She was trapped, utterly immobile within her body as electricity coursed through her muscles. Someone was moving her. Ashley put all her concentration into moving her arms and legs as she realized the woman was pulling her toward the now open door to the car.

"No!" she screamed, only she still wasn't sure it had come out. She felt as though she was yelling, but with her body unable to move, she didn't know if her mouth was functioning or not.

And then just as fast as it had begun, the force left her body and she went limp, her limbs working again. She shook her head and put her hands to the pavement. She was lying between the sidewalk and the car. If she could just get up. She could cry out, get a neighbor's attention. Anything.

She heard the woman swear, then felt pain as a hand grasped her hair. Her hands shot out to try to stop the blow, but it was too late. Her attacker slammed her head into the hard edge of the car door jam. And then her head began to swim, a fogginess taking her under. Sweeping her away. And she was gone.

CHAPTER TWENTY-TWO

P art of Ashley never wanted to wake up and another part screamed for her to open her eyes and see what she was facing. See what had happened. Because deep inside, she knew it was bad. Something had gone horribly wrong.

She didn't think she'd actually been unconscious for very long, but she'd had the sensation of not being able to move her arms or legs for a long time now. Slowly, she was becoming more lucid. The fog in her brain seemed to be lifting and she focused on sounds to try to pull herself further out of the mist. She remembered the hit to her head. Then she could remember vague flashes of her attacker stopping the car, binding her hands and feet, and gagging her. Then, nothing again.

Until she woke moments ago and began to process what was happening around her. The sound of the car engine, traffic like a highway. Her mouth was dry and she could feel something packed into it. Fabric of some kind, so she was only able to breathe through her nose. There was something holding the fabric in and by the way it pinched and pulled at her, she guessed it was tape of some kind.

She lay on the floorboards of the back seat of a car. Hands behind her back, bound tightly at the wrists. Ashley closed her eyes and willed herself to stay calm. Well, that wasn't right. First she had to get calm, then she could think about staying that way. Because she'd left the world of calm a while back. Her heart was racing and she was headed straight on into Panicsville at breakneck speed. And who could blame her?

She worked at the binding on her wrists for what seemed like hours. At one point, she began to thrash and make whatever noise she could through the gag, trying to get her attacker to talk to her, to...well, she really didn't know what. She just couldn't sit and do nothing as she was taken miles and miles from her home by a woman she didn't know.

It hadn't worked. The woman had turned on the radio, blasting it up high, and kept right on going. So, as tears fell and the radio blasted rock ballads from the past, Ashley listened to the car eat up miles and miles of road. She'd already been removed from the scene of the attack, and all she could think was how bad that was. Very bad. One of the first things you're taught in self-defense is not to allow your attacker to move you to a new location. To scream, to kick, to punch. To scratch and claw and bite.

But not ever let yourself be moved. And she'd failed miserably there.

She didn't know how much time passed before they left the highway and the road became rough, bouncing Ashley painfully. Every rut and bump they hit jarred her head, making the ache from where she'd been hit throb. She gritted her teeth and tried to push herself into the back seat of the car with her legs to brace against the motion. It helped a bit, but even that action was wearing on her already worn-out body.

The car slowed and she tracked the sounds of the engine cutting off, the front door opening and closing, then the door at her head opening.

"Get up." Someone smacked the top of her head and Ashley was unable to bring her arms up to block the hits. This was nothing like the pain she'd suffered when her head had been bouncing off the metal of the car doorjamb earlier, but the instinct to ward off any further damage was strong.

"Get out. We're going for a walk."

Ashley grunted and then immediately regretted it when the tape was ripped from her face and the gag pulled out. Her mouth was so dry, swallowing hurt, and her skin burned from the removal of the tape. She rolled to her stomach and tried to swallow, but all she felt was a sharp pain under her tongue and her arms screaming in pain from being bound for so long.

Finally she spoke, her voice scratchy. "I can't get up with my arms like this. I can't move."

There was a lot of noise in the trunk and then she felt

cold metal on her wrists and tried to stay still. After several minutes, her arms were freed and she was dragged to the seat. The woman tossed a dull-looking knife onto her lap.

"Cut the tape on your ankles."

Her brain raced as she tried to figure out what to do. She knew a lot about getting out of situations like this, and yet, with all her knowledge gained from researching her books, she still drew a complete blank. Her brain wasn't functioning at all. She looked at the woman and saw she held a small gun in her hands.

She knew from her research smaller didn't necessarily mean less damage if she was shot. She thought she should be able to remember the name of the gun, but the only way to describe what she was feeling was stupid. She felt like someone had shut her brain off or turned a dial down on its power somehow. Like she was operating at half capacity.

The heroines in her books always managed to do the right thing. To somehow keep the person distracted while they came up with a brilliant plan to escape. And here she was, hardly able to form a sentence and certainly unable to move, with the pain shooting through her legs as they returned from their numb state.

She began to saw at the duct tape around her ankles and was able to free them fairly readily. She looked up at the woman.

"Toss it over the front seat," she said, with a nod of her head.

Ashley looked at the knife. The thing was so freaking rusted and dull, it probably wouldn't have done her much good anyway, but giving it up almost physically hurt. She threw it over the front seat, feeling a deep ache at the utter lack of hope she felt.

"Who are you?" She took a better look at the woman. Or she tried to. There wasn't much light being cast from the interior of the car. She thought back to the few moments she'd seen the woman outside her house earlier. Shoulder-length hair that had been dyed black but was showing light brown roots at the base. Squinting now, she could make out a plain face and eyes that looked a little too panicked for Ashley's comfort. Like the woman was just a smidge on the wrong side of crazy.

She waved the gun around a little. "Get out. We have to get started." She looked up at the sky and Ashley saw it was full dark out. That meant it was somewhere well after nine o'clock at night, she would guess. Which meant they'd driven for several hours, at least. She'd left the library at six o'clock.

How had she been out for so long? Ashley felt a rising panic as she brought her hand to her head. What she felt made her want to crumple in a heap on the ground. She didn't know much about head injuries, but it felt bad. There was a large knot on the side of her head—somewhere between a golf ball and baseball in size—and she could feel blood caked and crusted in her hair, but also warm blood still coming slowly down one side of her face.

Being unconscious, bleeding for so long—those could not be good signs. Before she could process any of this, Crazy Chick was talking again. "Who am I? I'm the woman whose life you just destroyed and didn't even give a thought to with your fake accusations. It's not nice to lie, you know. Not nice at all. And you and I are going to find a way to fix this. We're going to find a way to undo what you've done."

Ashley stared at the woman. Clearly she was unbalanced. Ashley couldn't for the life of her figure out what the woman was talking about. She hadn't accused anyone of anything, she thought, before the realization crashed into her. Of course she had. This woman was talking about Bill Franks. But surely the fact that there was a skeleton in his backyard—and not the figurative kind—meant this woman couldn't possibly think Ashley's accusation was false.

That level of denial didn't seem possible. But Ashley remembered Garret telling her that Franks' girlfriend had denied the truth of the molestation charges. That she'd refused to take her daughter from his home, even with the possibility that he might be released pending the trial.

"Get out of the damned car," the woman screeched with another shake of the gun as she literally stomped her foot. Ashley's suspicion that the woman was walking a mental tightrope was confirmed. Seriously unbalanced.

Ashley stepped from the car, not sure her legs would hold her. They did, but were still stiff and not feeling very strong. She looked around as her eyes adjusted to the darkness and realized there was some light coming from the nearly full moon above. She still couldn't be sure where she was. The area was wooded and they seemed to have pulled into a small shallow at the side of the road. It couldn't be described as a parking lot. More like a parking area for one or two cars at most.

Wherever they were, it wasn't a main hiking area, that's for sure. It gave new meaning to the phrase, "off the beaten path." If they were in one of the state parks between Evers and Austin, they weren't in a heavily travelled part. Ashley remembered that there were some more remote areas at the back of Inks Lake State Park and wondered if that's where they were. That or one of another six or so possibilities. Granite Shoals, maybe? She wanted to groan as she ran through all of the places they could be.

Her thoughts ran to Garret. She'd give anything to be safe in his arms, but he would be out with his friends all night. And she'd insisted he didn't need to drive to her house that night. So he'd have no reason to notice her missing until tomorrow at the earliest. The library was closed on Sundays, so no one would expect her to show up for work the following day either. Her family would expect her for dinner, at least. So the earliest someone would notice her missing was tomorrow evening.

She casually dropped a hand to her pants to see if her phone was in her pocket. Not there. And apparently not casually enough.

"Don't worry." Crazy Chick held up Ashley's phone. "I texted lover boy. Sent kisses and said goodnight. He won't be expecting to hear from you again." She was almost cheerful. It was eerie.

Ashley took a deep breath, but wasn't able to say anything before Crazy Chick spoke again.

"Now we have to walk from here. Let's go." The woman clicked on a heavy-duty flashlight and pointed its beam to an opening in the woods. If she hadn't pointed to it, Ashley never would have realized there was an overgrown trail there. It was narrow and covered with trees and branches. It wasn't a path they were likely to run into anyone on, even if it had been daytime.

The thought of entering these woods in the dark was terrifying. Doing so at gunpoint with an unhinged lunatic as her guide? Well, that plain sucked. But Ashley couldn't think of any way out of it. If she ran, she could be shot. If she tried to fight the woman, she could be shot. The only thing she could think to do was to go along with her. To try to talk to her. To either gain a foothold to reason with her, or just buy time for some opening to act. Or for Garret to get to her.

How on earth she thought Garret would find her was a mystery, but she held out hope. At least if she stayed alive, he had a shot at it. She stepped onto the path.

"Where are we headed?" Ashley walked carefully, watching for branches or roots in the path as best she could. She wasn't dressed for this. She had on slacks and a blouse with casual ballerina flats that slipped off her feet easily while at the library. On a hiking trail? They were like a written invitation to a twisted ankle.

"An old cabin," the woman answered simply enough.

"Do I get to know your name?"

"Michelle."

Ashley glanced back over her shoulder, but saw

Michelle hadn't lowered the gun. "And what are you hoping we can do out at this cabin?" *Not that I'm at all sure I want to know.*

"Just keep going. We need to get there and get off the trail."

Because someone might see us out here?

Ashley actually laughed. No one would see them. There was no need to rush. Especially since she wasn't at all sure Michelle wouldn't kill her as soon as they got there. Hell, for all Ashley knew, the woman had pre-dug her grave out at this cabin. And just like that, Ashley was picturing digging her own grave at gunpoint next to an abandoned cabin in the woods. *Fabulous.* For the first time, thinking like a writer wasn't fun. Not fun at all.

GARRET LET himself into his apartment after two in the morning. He probably shouldn't have had so much to drink, but he'd decided as long as he wasn't making the drive to Ashley's, he might as well relax and enjoy himself. It had been a long time since he'd gone out with the guys. And he'd done the right thing and hitched a ride home, leaving his car at the bar for the night.

He looked at the clock and considered texting Ashley, but thought better of it. She'd be in bed and he didn't want to wake her. Walking to his bedroom, he couldn't help but scan the living room and the kitchen as he passed by them.

They were plain. Serviceable. A man's apartment for sure. A man who obviously lived alone.

He continued down the hall to his room and shucked his jeans and shirt before sliding into the bed. What he'd once thought was a great bed now seemed empty. Pretty lonely, in fact. He liked slipping between Ashley's sheets much better. And it wasn't the fact that her sheets were softer or that she had all those fluffy pillows or the pretty headboard. He couldn't care less about those things. It was Ashley. Her soft body curled up against his. The way she'd toss a leg over him or turn and snuggle that sweet ass of hers into his groin as she slept. The way he could wake her with his hands or mouth or—

He groaned. He needed to stop. All the alcohol he'd drunk wasn't enough to dampen his libido, as evidenced by the raging hard-on he now sported. But it was enough to keep him from getting in the car and going to see her. Letting his mind explore her body in his imagination sure as hell wasn't helpful. He tossed a pillow over his head, shut his eyes, and tried to think about something else.

But when he'd managed to force his mind from Ashley's curves, he was left thinking about how much fuller his life had been since she'd stepped into his world. And how much more he liked the nights when he was with her. How much more like a home her house felt. And not because she had photos and knickknacks or whatever they were. It was her. It was the fact that her smile and laughter filled the space.

He rolled over and grabbed his phone and scrolled to her last few text messages, reading them with a grin. He'd see her tomorrow and make up for tonight. He turned off his phone and put his hands behind his head, thinking about Ashley and all the ways she made his world a little better. He was pretty sure he fell asleep with that dumb ass grin on his face.

CHAPTER TWENTY-THREE

G arret's morning was shot to hell before he even woke up. Doug called, dragging him from a deep sleep.

"Yeah?"

"Captain just called. Got a 10-56A out in Burnet, but there might be signs of foul play. He wants us to take this one since Ganley is out this week." *Attempted suicide.* Those were never fun. He supposed it was better than a suicide that had been successful.

"Okay. Coroner on the way?" Garret stood and pulled on the jeans he'd worn the night before, then thought better of it. He'd been in a smoky bar for much of the night. He pulled them off, put on a pair of black slacks, t-shirt, and shoulder holster.

"En route."

"Any ID?" Garret was asking because they both knew if they had an ID, that might mean there were family or friends present, and that always made these things hard. Especially with a suicide attempt. They could be exceedingly messy and hard for family members to witness.

"None yet. Young woman. Late twenties, early thirties. She hung herself from a tree. Unconscious when she was discovered. It didn't sound like they thought she would make it through the next twenty-four hours. Now you know as much as I do," Doug said and hung up the phone.

Garret finished his morning routine, which was short and efficient, then left to meet Doug at the location his partner had texted him. He wasn't looking forward to this. No matter who the woman was, when someone took their own life, it was never an easy scene to process. There were too many "what ifs" and "if onlys"—what if she'd just reached out to someone? If only someone had been with her instead of her being alone. If only she'd hung on just one more hour. Just one more day.

He let himself out the door and hung up, bracing against the task in front of him. This was shaping up to be an extremely shitty day.

CORA KNOCKED AGAIN but Ashley didn't answer the door. Her car was in the driveway. Knowing Ashley, she had walked over to the diner to meet someone for breakfast. Ashley's little house was close enough to town that she often walked wherever she needed to go.

Cora used her key to let herself in and grabbed a cold

glass of water. She had biked over and still needed to bike the four miles back. She scribbled a note to Ashley, telling her to call when she got home, and let herself back out the door. She wanted to see if she could catch a ride up to their parents' house later that afternoon for dinner. Not because she really needed a ride. She simply hadn't been seeing as much of her sister since the hot cop had come along, and she missed her. Hopefully, Ashley would call and they could have coffee before going out to see the rest of the family for dinner.

She hopped on her bike and pedaled off, determined to make it home before ten when the Texas heat would make biking unbearably hot. But when she drove by the house a few hours later and pulled in the driveway, she couldn't help but wonder if Ashley had come home yet. It was almost two o'clock and Ashley hadn't called, despite Cora's note from that morning, but her car was still in the driveway.

She remembered a few weeks ago when Garret had found Ashley huddled in the closet, and a small bit of worry formed in her belly. But Ashley had been doing really well lately. And surely when Cora had come in the house that morning, if Ashley had been upset or sick or something like that, she'd have called out to Cora.

Cora let herself into the house and checked the bedroom. No sign of Ashley. She looked on the kitchen counter and found her note right where she'd left it. She pulled her phone from her pocket and texted Ashley.

Hey, where are you?

It took several minutes before she got an answer. She had a feeling Ashley would tell her she was with the hot cop, as Cora liked to refer to him. They'd been spending a lot of time together lately. Cora almost felt a little awkward, like maybe she shouldn't have bothered them. Who knew? Maybe Ashley had spent the night at Garret's house and they were still in bed late into the afternoon. Her phone beeped with an incoming text.

Just at the library working.

Cora frowned. She'd driven by the library a minute before and it was dark. As dark as it should be, since it was closed on Sundays. And Cora knew perfectly well Ashley didn't go in to work on her day off. She worked hard. She loved her library and often went the extra mile for it, but she didn't work on Sundays. Cora swallowed her disappointment at the lie and texted back a quick, *ok c u later* message before leaving Ashley's and locking up.

She was bothered and couldn't help but wonder why Ashley felt she needed to lie instead of just letting Cora know she was with Garret. Maybe Ashley felt the need to lie since Cora wasn't dating anyone. Hadn't had a date in over a year. Had no hope or prayer of a date for the foreseeable future.

And now she felt fan-freaking-tastic. Cora pulled out of the driveway and decided to head to her parents' house early. Maybe her mom would let her be her taster in the kitchen like she had when Cora was younger. Then she could feel like a desperate lonely woman who was also destined to be a ginormous woman in a tent dress ten years down the road.

Fabulous.

GARRET LOOKED at the clock on the wall and rubbed a hand down his face. His day had gone from shitty to worse and back again. They'd arrived on scene at the attempted suicide, to find out the victim had been admitted to the ICU unit and, if she survived at all, she'd likely have brain damage. She might never wake up. The doctors hadn't let them in to see her, but since she wasn't conscious there wasn't much they could do there anyway. They asked for a crime scene technician to be permitted to fingerprint her so an identification could be made and the family notified.

They'd processed the scene and found what could be evidence of a struggle, or could have been the victim's own footprints as she struggled to set up the log she'd tipped over to facilitate her hanging. They'd collected as much evidence as possible, given what little there was, but for now, their priority remained finding family and friends who could answer questions and help lead to more information.

Next, they'd had to drive half an hour outside Branson Falls to process a burglary. That case ended up matching several other cases in the statewide system, so they'd spent a few hours on the phone trying to track down details of cases in other jurisdictions to figure out if they were truly related.

They'd topped it off by finding out one of their cases from a few months ago might be tossed out of court due to some errors in processing evidence over at the state lab. They'd be scrambling to see if they could find any further evidence to back the case if the original evidence got thrown out. But at several months out from the crime, finding anything new was a stretch.

Garret was surprised to see it was four o'clock and he hadn't heard from Ashley all day. Not since she'd returned his text this morning. He hoped that didn't mean her day was turning out to be as bad as his. He knew she planned to work on her new book today. Maybe she got so buried in her writing, she hadn't noticed the time.

Hey gorgeous, miss me?

He waited with a stupid grin on his face, expecting some kind of comeback having to do with Johnny Depp sweeping her off her feet or something. He got nothing. And nothing again when he texted twenty minutes later.

"Everything okay?" Doug asked, looking up from where he'd been working on the last of the reports they needed to file before taking off for the day.

Garret frowned. "Just can't reach Ashley. No biggie," he said with a shrug. He didn't want to look like a lovesick goon in front of Doug, but man, he wished he'd hear from her. He wanted nothing more than to drive to her house and climb into bed with her. "It's probably nothing. She eats dinner at her parents' house every Sunday." He glanced back at the clock. Four-thirty. Maybe she went over there early and was busy with her family.

Part of him felt like a pansy for caring that she hadn't

called. For wondering if she was pulling away from him since she'd insisted he not come over last night, and didn't seem all that eager to see him or talk to him today. But hell if he wasn't just a little worried about that.

Doug laughed at his partner. "Oh, she's got you good, my man. She's got you good."

"Good how?" Garret was feeling pretty defensive at the moment and it came through in his tone. Doug laughed harder. A couple of the other guys in the precinct wandered over and Garret had to sit and listen to Doug describe how desperate Garret was for Ashley's attention. How he was texting her day and night like a pimply faced kid.

Garret ignored them, but the words ate at him, because it was true. And he had a bad feeling that Ashley was avoiding him. Like maybe he'd come on too strong or was more into this than she was. He had thought there was something real starting between them. But maybe for her this had just been about sex and she was done with him now. Plenty of women had a thing for cops. Maybe she was just another badge bunny and she was done with him now that he'd given her what she wanted.

But no. That didn't make sense. She hadn't even been intimate with a man in years. She wouldn't just hop into bed with him and then move on. Would she?

"Hey, you all right, man? I was just screwing with you."

Garret looked up to see that the rest of the group had walked away and his partner was now watching him intently. He shook his head. "Yeah, I'm good. Just need to go catch up on sleep."

Doug nodded. "You go ahead and take off. I'm almost done here. I'll take care of these," he said, gesturing to the reports he had been working on.

"Thanks. I appreciate it," he said as he pushed in his chair and straightened a few things on his desk. He didn't like the fact that he was feeling much too raw at what seemed like rejection from Ashley. Hell, he didn't even like that he was taking this as a rejection. So she hadn't texted or called as often as she usually did. So she'd wanted him to have a guys' night out last night. He was taking this way too personally.

"See you in the morning. We can go over to the hospital and see if the doctor will let us see our Jane Doe. See if there's been any change in her condition," Doug said, and Garret was reminded that things could be worse. Somewhere, someone was likely missing this poor woman, worried to death for her, but unable to find her. He gave a nod as he walked away. He should stop being a whiny baby and suck it up. Just go talk to Ashley. Find out where things stood. Because if she wasn't on the same page with him, if she didn't see this going someplace serious between them, he needed to find out now while he could still walk away without committing his heart.

Shit. Who was he kidding? His heart *was* committed. Had been for a while with her. And if she didn't feel the same way about him, it was going to suck trying to walk away unscathed.

CHAPTER TWENTY-FOUR

Cora drove through town after running to the grocery store. She had decided she would head over to her mom's after she went and grabbed the ingredients for apple pie. If she was going to be wearing tent dresses, she might as well go for broke and have a slice of pie. Or twenty.

Her route took her back past Ashley's house and she was surprised to see Garret walking up to the front door. When he rang the bell, she pulled over to the side of the road and shut off her car, a strange feeling prickling at the base of her neck.

She'd been so sure Ashley had been lying to her about where she was because she was with Garret. If her sister wasn't with Garret and she wasn't at the library, where was she? And why had she lied to Cora about it?

"Garret?" she called out as she walked up the front walk. "She's not home. I thought for sure she was with you."

His gaze swung to Ashley's car in the driveway, before he looked back to Cora. "I haven't seen her all day."

Cora felt her stomach sink and she pulled her phone out again to text Ashley. "When I texted her earlier, she told me she was at the library working, but I knew that wasn't true. It was dark and closed up when I passed it a few moments before that." She spoke almost absently now as she sent an urgent text to Ashley asking her to call her. "I thought she was lying because she'd slept at your house or something and didn't want to tell me."

Garret didn't like the feeling that was creeping over him, like a cold wet towel had been thrown over his shoulders. "Is it normal for her to lie to you like that?" He asked the question but he knew the answer before she shook her head. The sisters were close. Ashley wouldn't lie without a reason.

Cora had dialed the phone now and she was listening but shaking her head. "Straight to voicemail."

Damn. If her cellphone was off, they would only be able to see what cell tower it pinged before shutting down. Who knows how far she might have travelled since it shut down or died. Doug had put in a call to start the process, but getting info from her cell phone might not matter now.

"When was the last time you talked to her or saw her?"

Cora continued to look at her phone while she answered, as if hoping to hear from her sister any moment. "Last night."

He thought about the text he'd gotten from Ashley that morning and the feeling of unease intensified. He could understand it if Ashley was avoiding him. They hadn't been together very long and maybe things had moved too quickly for her. But why would she lie to Cora?

His mind flashed to the Jane Doe they had sitting in the hospital waiting for her family to find her, but he shook off the thought. Ashley was fine. She was just—just what? Damn, he had no idea. But he wouldn't panic yet.

"Why don't you call your parents and your siblings and see if they've heard from her. Maybe text a few friends. I don't think it's time to panic yet," he said. But when Cora turned back to her phone to do just that, he took out his own phone and scrolled through the contacts. He didn't know the identity of the Jane Doe and he hadn't laid eyes on her himself yet, but her description suddenly sounded too much like Ashley.

He repeated his pep talk in his head, telling him that the young woman with dark hair and a small build wasn't Ashley. It wasn't. But he texted a friend on staff at the hospital anyway and asked for a photo of the woman in the ICU. He told his friend it was urgent, even as he told himself he was being foolish.

It's not her. It's not her. It's not her.

Over and over, he forced the thought as Cora shook her head again.

"No one has heard from her."

"Do you have a key?" he asked Cora and she nodded, walking up the few steps to the door.

"I came inside earlier to see if she was here and leave her a note. I thought maybe she was sick," she said over her shoulder as they walked in the front door. "I checked the whole house. She isn't here."

He checked himself but didn't see anything out of the ordinary. His phone chimed and he said a prayer as he lifted it to look at the image his friend had sent.

Christ, he'd never been so relieved in his life. The woman in the photo had a tube running down her throat and a face as white as the sheets she lay on, but he could tell it wasn't Ashley. Thank God, it wasn't Ashley.

"What's that? Is that her?" Cora asked him.

"No. Just something for a case. It's not important now. Is there anyone else you can think to call?"

"I texted the people she spends any amount of time with, and all of my family. We all assumed she'd be at the house in a couple of hours for dinner, but haven't heard from her."

Garret stepped out on the front porch, scanning the neighborhood, while Cora stood behind him, shifting from one foot to the other. He turned to look back at her and nodded to his left.

"You go check with the neighbors down that way, I'll check to the right."

"Okay," she said.

"Hey, Cora, don't worry. She's probably fine." He smiled at her and she offered a small smile back, but he had a feeling she didn't believe it any more than he did. His gut was screaming at him. Something was wrong. He just didn't know what.

CHAPTER TWENTY-FIVE

Michelle looked down at the phone on the floor. She'd been answering texts, pretending to be Ashley, right up until it died hours earlier. She paced the length of the cabin floor, before swinging back again. Bill should have been here to help her with this. She shouldn't have had to do this on her own. And now, things were an absolute clusterfuck. She'd screwed it up. She should have made it look like an accident, but there was no way to do that now. She was in way over her head and she knew it.

"Damn it!"

"Maybe if we talk about it, I can help you work it out," Ashley said quietly, hoping it was the right move. They'd walked for over an hour and had been in this crappy, broken-down cabin for most of the night. Ashley hadn't dared sleep. While they had trudged through the woods, she had tried to get Michelle to talk, to answer questions, but the woman had resisted and shoved Ashley forward. Ashley's feet were killing her and she had twisted her ankle at one point. The swelling wasn't too bad yet, and the pain took her focus off the pain in her head, but she wasn't exactly confident she could run, if given the chance.

Michelle had seemed to get more and more agitated throughout the night, talking to herself and even hitting the side of her head a few times with her open hand. As the night turned into day and the morning had passed, Ashley had watched Michelle and debated every possible course of action she could think of. There weren't many.

Ashley was taking a gamble, trying to get her to talk again. Who knew if she'd end up provoking the woman, or if she'd somehow find a way to get through to her?

For the better part of the last few hours, Ashley had inched her way toward the wall to the back of the cabin, where a few pieces of shattered glass lay beneath one of the few windows in the place. Now that she'd slipped the largest piece she could find into her right hand, she felt slightly more comfortable drawing Michelle's focus back to her.

"I'm a good listener, Michelle. If you'll just let me listen, I'm sure we can figure this out together." Ashley wished momentarily that she'd researched Hostage Negotiation 101 or something for one of her books. That would have come in handy right now. She wondered what Garret would do. What would he tell her to do? Probably stay calm. That was becoming more and more difficult as things progressed.

Michelle turned toward her, and seemed to realize Ashley was talking to her. "What did you say?"

Ashley took a long breath. "I said I'm a good listener. Maybe we can work this out together if you let me know what's going on."

"What's going on? What's going on is I'm alone! This wasn't supposed to happen like this. Bill was supposed to be the one. He was supposed to be it. The man who would marry me and take care of me. Of *me*!" She whacked herself pretty firmly on the chest when she said this, and Ashley struggled not to flinch. Or laugh. Because if she did laugh, she had a feeling it would be the hysterical laughter of a woman on the edge who might have just pushed another woman on the edge right over the damned cliff.

"You're not alone. I'm here."

"That's the problem. You. You're the problem."

Great. Ashley apparently sucked at the whole negotiate-with-the-hostage-taker thing. This was a fine time to figure that out.

"You want to know what the problem is?" Now Michelle's focus was fully on Ashley and she was waving that gun around again, her finger most definitely on the trigger. Ashley stifled the urge to tell her she was supposed to keep her finger along the trigger guard when not taking aim. That probably wouldn't help matters.

She remained silent as Michelle continued. "Your false accusations have put the man I love in jail and now I need to take care of you to see that he gets out. It's not like I haven't done it before. I have, you know. I can do this. It's just that it changes you, you know? And, the last time, I didn't plan it. I didn't have to think about it ahead of time."

Ashley didn't want to know what she was talking about, because she had a sinking feeling Michelle was talking about Alice. That this woman had been the one to kill Alice, not Bill Franks. Which made sense. Alice never would have let Bill Franks into her apartment willingly, yet there hadn't been a sign of a struggle or forced entry. Alice had been making tea when her attacker had stabbed her in the back.

Ashley hated to think that Alice had trusted this woman, had let her into her home only to be killed by her. But she knew Alice. If Alice knew a child was in trouble, she'd do whatever it took to help them. If Michelle had shown up claiming she wanted to talk, Alice might have let her guard down. She might even have let Michelle enter her home when anyone working in social services knew that wasn't wise.

"You killed Alice?" she asked quietly. The look that came over Michelle's face confused Ashley. It was one of regret, despite the fact that apparently she seemed to be trying to work up the courage to do the same thing to Ashley.

"She didn't leave me any choice," Michelle said, with the conviction of one who had justice and right behind her words. "She kept trying to convince me to leave Bill. Said he liked to do dirty things to little girls and my Evie was in danger if we stayed with him. She wouldn't stop."

Michelle turned away now, pacing again, and she

seemed to be in conversation more with herself than with Ashley. Ashley gripped the glass in her hand and moved her arm to sit beside her leg on the floor. The shard would still be out of Michelle's sight but she felt more ready to act when there was an opening.

"I told her, he never touched Evie. He wanted *me*. If he liked little girls he wouldn't be able to get it up for me the way he did. He wouldn't like the things I did to him." She turned to Ashley again, as if pleading for her to support her side of the argument. "She just kept babbling about some non-something. Non-exclusion, non-exclusive. Something about him liking grown women and young girls both. She said she could get me proof and she's all chatty and making me tea, and trying to be my friend. But she wasn't my friend. She was trying to get in between me and Bill. And I just couldn't let her do that." She threw up her hands, gun and all, and Ashley again watched in horror as she waved that hand around with her finger firmly on the trigger.

Before Ashley could respond, Michelle narrowed her eyes at her. The conversation was decidedly one-way at this point, and Ashley wanted to try to slow things down, but she couldn't get a word in. Michelle took another step toward Ashley and she gripped the glass shard more tightly, getting ready. She felt its bite on her skin, but that didn't matter. She'd cut herself in the process of using it against Michelle, for sure, but that couldn't be helped.

"You're not my friend, either." Michelle took another step, then another, as she raged. She was almost upon

Ashley now, but she wasn't close enough for Ashley to use the glass. If she fired that gun before she got closer, this could all very well be over without Ashley having a chance at defending herself.

"You're not my friend! You want me to talk to you, to open up, but you're the one making these accusations against Bill. You're the reason they took him away from me. It's you!"

Ashley's heart was pounding and it felt like it had crawled right up her throat. She held her breath, waiting. Praying Michelle wouldn't just stand at a distance and empty that gun into her.

Michelle suddenly slowed. "I took the file from Alice's house. She had all these notes and your name was in there so I went to see you. I thought maybe I could scare you off."

The rat, Ashley realized, but she kept her mouth shut.

"I watched, trying to figure out what would make Bill want you. I dyed my hair black and got a pair of reading glasses. But you know what? He didn't like it. He hated it. He didn't want *you*. He wanted *me*." She was screeching now. "He wanted *me*!"

And then Michelle rushed forward, one hand out as if to grab at Ashley, but Ashley held her ground. Waiting. Waiting. At the last possible minute, she clutched the glass shard. It cut deep into her hand, the warmth of blood spilling down her wrist. She brought her arm down hard, not really having much aim as she tried to ignore the pain slicing through her hand. She didn't process the stunned look on Michelle's face as she threw herself forward.

The women went down and Ashley heard the gun fly, skittering across the floor. She pulled the glass back and thrust again, trying not to watch as it sank into Michelle's neck. There was blood everywhere and Ashley didn't know how much of it was Michelle's and how much was hers.

She left the glass embedded in Michelle's still form, and bolted for the front of the cabin, bursting through the door and running into the woods. She didn't know if Michelle was dead or alive, and she didn't know if she would be able to pursue Ashley or not. She thought briefly that she should have picked up the gun, but being new at this whole fleeing the scene of her attack, she imagined she'd done more than one or two things wrong.

As she tried to wade and climb through the tangled underbrush of the woods, she realized mistake number two. She should have taken the time to orient herself and find the path they'd taken to the cabin. She stopped and sucked in some deep breaths, bending at the waist to stop the dizziness in her head. Her ankle throbbed and her hand was bleeding heavily. Enough to make her stomach flip as she looked at it. Ashley took off the cardigan she'd worn to work the previous day. It would be too bulky to wrap around her hand. She removed the matching silk shell and folded it lengthwise a few times, then wrapped it tightly around her hand, tucking the edge in as best she could with only her teeth and one hand. She put the cardigan back on and looked around.

The cabin was no longer in sight. She listened for several minutes, but didn't hear the sounds of Michelle following her. But there weren't any other sounds either. No sounds of people talking or a road or water. She was distinctly aware that she hadn't eaten since lunch the day before and hadn't had anything to drink since around the same time. She'd had a little water in the afternoon at the library, but not as much as she should have. She wondered how long it would be before she felt the effects of that. Add in the blood loss, the twisted ankle, and the lack of sleep, and she didn't want to think about her body's condition at the moment.

She closed her eyes and pictured the cabin. When they had come out of the trail last night, they'd been on the left side of the cabin. The south side. She was fairly sure of that much, at least. When she came out after stabbing Michelle, she'd run straight out the front of the cabin and into the woods. Once she'd hit the woods, she tried to go straight, but she wasn't sure she really had. Climbing around trees and brush made the trajectory a little iffy, at best.

But even if she had gone straight, that was the wrong direction. She looked around. Looked up and tried to figure out which way was south. She realized she didn't have a clue. They'd travelled mostly uphill last night, but now the terrain seemed to be fairly flat. She turned in a slow circle, trying to gauge if there was a slant to the ground at all.

Yes. There was definitely a slight downhill slant in one direction. Which meant that should be south. Toward the road. Toward where they'd left the car. Not that she had keys to it, but maybe she could figure out how to hotwire it. She hadn't been a model kid as a teen, but unfortunately, she'd never learned how to hotwire a car. Maybe she could wing it. *Sure.* Just like she could wing the survival skills needed to find south. She rolled her eyes at herself, raised her hand up to her shoulder to try to slow the bleeding, and set off in the direction she'd chosen. At the very least, she would commit to one direction and keep moving.

CHAPTER TWENTY-SIX

"I'm sorry I can't be more help. I didn't see who the woman was," the neighbor diagonally across the street from Ashley's house told Garret. "I just saw Ashley walk up to her next to a blue car, and then one of my kids called to me and I went into the den. That's at the back of the house. When I came back to the kitchen, I think they were gone."

She scrunched up her face as though thinking and pointed toward one of the windows on the front of her house. "That window is right over my kitchen sink. I was getting dinner ready. I don't remember seeing them there when I drained the pasta, but I'm not really sure if I looked at the window then or not. I was really just focused on getting dinner ready."

"Do you know what kind of car it was?"

The woman shook her head decisively at that. "I'm not good with things like make and model. I wouldn't know a

Honda from a Ford. But it was a sedan. Smallish. That's about all I can tell you."

"Would you mind showing me where the car was parked?" Garret asked.

"Sure," she said and stepped farther out onto her porch. She pointed across the street. "It was right in front of that little tree. Maybe a little ahead of it, but somewhere around there," she said as she gestured to the small tree in Ashley's yard.

"Thank you," Garret said, handing her his card. "If you think of anything else, please let me know." He'd said the words so many other times in cases. Today, he meant them in a way he never had before. He desperately wanted the woman to remember more about what she'd seen. She'd said she didn't know the woman and Ashley had seemed like she'd walked up willingly. She didn't witness an argument or fight, but then, she'd only seen them for a few seconds before she'd moved away from the window.

Garret jogged down the steps and across to Ashley's, where Cora stood waiting for him.

"Did she see something?" she asked.

"Yeah," he said. "She saw Ashley talking to a woman about Ashley's age. Dark hair. A small blue sedan."

He walked to the sidewalk in front of the tree and looked around.

"Shit." He bit off the string of curses he wanted to let loose. There was a foot-wide spot of blood on the gravel road next to the curb. It looked sticky enough to be fairly fresh. Not within hours, but certainly within the last day or so. He looked up as Cora approached.

"Is that—" She gripped her stomach. "Oh God, that's not blood, is it?"

"I'm afraid so. We don't know it's hers, though." He took out his phone and called Doug. He needed to know if Bill Franks was still in custody or if he'd made bail. And he needed to know the make and model of Franks' car and of Michelle Davis's car. Technically, he probably didn't have enough to open a missing person's case on Ashley. But that didn't mean he couldn't call in every favor and every connection he had to be sure she was safe.

As he was making phone calls, Ashley's family members began to arrive, and the neighbors all came out to see what was going on. He questioned everyone, even the neighbors he'd already talked to. He needed to find someone who had seen who Ashley had been with yesterday. If that person had taken her, they were coming up on twenty-four hours missing, a fact that made his gut churn. How the fuck had it taken him twenty-four hours to realize she was missing?

He looked at his messages. If she was taken by the woman the neighbor had seen, the last few texts he'd gotten from Ashley's phone had been sent by someone else. Someone who had her phone, and likely had her. Someone who, hopefully, hadn't hurt her yet. The odds were against her right now, but he would cling to that hope. He'd cling to anything. Because he wanted Ashley in his life, in his world. In his heart.

CHAPTER TWENTY-SEVEN

G arret was quickly losing his mind. They had virtually nothing to go on. They'd gotten a picture of Michelle Davis and shown it to the neighbor who had seen Ashley the night before. She said it could have been the woman, but she wasn't certain. Michelle Davis did drive a blue sedan so they had put out a BOLO to all law enforcement in the county and several surrounding counties for the vehicle.

"I hate to say it," Garret said quietly to Doug as he watched Cora cry. Ashley's sister was on the couch with her mom on one side and one of her brothers on the other. She was blaming herself for not realizing Ashley was in trouble sooner. Yeah, welcome to the club on that one. "I think we should interview the girl."

Doug raised his eyebrows. "Evie Davis?"

"Yeah." Garret nodded. "We don't have anything else to

go on. We need something. Anything. Maybe she can give us a clue as to where her mom might have taken Ashley."

Bill Franks was still in prison, but Michelle had visited him several times and the only theory they had was that she was going after Ashley to help him. They hadn't found any other motivation for anyone else to have grabbed her, and it just didn't feel like a random kidnapping to Garret. Doug frowned at him. Garret knew questioning the child wasn't going to be a popular move, but they needed to find something to go on. Anything.

His partner raised his phone and began to scroll through his contacts. "Let me see if the caseworker can go over and talk to her, find out anything about where they were living before Franks' or anyplace they spent time."

Garret felt the muscles in his jaw tense but he nodded. He'd let them start with the caseworker questioning Evie, but if they didn't get anywhere, he'd go talk to Michelle Davis's daughter himself. He needed something to go on here.

He felt the tension build and looked around, angry with himself for not having a single damned lead. Ashley was out there with God knew what being done to her, most likely terrified, possibly hurt. He couldn't even begin to let himself think about the alternative. That she might be dead before he could reach her. He wouldn't go there. *Couldn't* go there.

"Hey," Doug said, with the kind of pointed look that had brought the man from the category of partner, to mentor, to brother. "We work the case. Just like any other.

We look at every angle, chase every lead. We just work the case. It's all we can do."

"Yeah," Garret said, but his teeth were still clenched tightly together and his body felt like it could snap in half if he moved wrong, he was wound so damned tight. He knew he needed to keep his head on straight for this or he'd make a mistake, overlook something, but damned if that wasn't the hardest thing he had to do. He needed to be *doing* and right now, he was just waiting.

They had the sheriff's office here to help, a search and rescue dog on standby, and a BOLO out on Michelle Davis and her vehicle. But other than the BOLO, there wasn't anything they could do.

It was another thirty nerve-wracking minutes before they got a call from the caseworker, and Garret had to admit, he was surprised to hear back that soon. He thought for sure he'd have to call and push to get answers. The worker must have driven straight over to interview Evie when they asked, and Garret knew he owed her for that. The people who worked for child services were overbooked and understaffed, and dropping everything to get them information meant something.

Doug put the phone on speaker after Doug, the sheriff, and Garret had stepped away from the group. Sheriff John Davies had a great deal of knowledge about the surrounding area and they were grateful to have his help. Besides, he was married to a woman who was good friends with Ashley. He was almost as motivated as Garret to get her back safely.

"Evie didn't have much to say. I can keep trying to talk

227

to her, but she said one thing that I thought you could start looking into," said the caseworker. "She said she and her mom slept in an old cabin for a couple of weeks before they moved in with Bill Franks. The way she talks about it, they were squatting and the place sounds abandoned and isolated."

The words isolated sliced at Garret's heart. He pictured Ashley alone and hurting and frightened in a place where no one would happen on her to help. And where he had very little hope of tracking her down.

"Any idea where it was?" He asked the question they were all thinking.

"She isn't sure, but she says they had to hike into it for a long time and she never saw anyone else around there. She would see other people when they drove in. There would be people camping and stuff, but then nothing for a while and nothing near where they stayed. She said the other people were camping at the crayon lake."

"Where?" John Davies asked, and Garret knew what he was thinking. There wasn't any place called Crayon Lake.

"I don't know," answered the worker. "I couldn't decipher it either, but I thought you guys might. She said her mom called it something and she can't remember the name. But, to her, it sounded like crayons. Or, her mom said it was like crayons. She wasn't sure."

The men looked at each other for a few long minutes before the sheriff raised his brows and leaned toward the phone that Doug still held on speaker between them. "Can you ask her if she means Inks Lake? It's got a lot of camping and hiking in the park but there's also a more isolated area in the back of the park that's pretty rough, not cared for or maintained at the moment. There are no open trails up that way, and I could see a cabin being hidden up there."

"Hang on," answered the caseworker, and they heard some muffled comments in the background. "Yes, that's it," she said when she came back on the line. "She says they used to drive by Inks Lake before hiking in to the cabin. I tried to see if she remembers anything about where they parked to hike, but she doesn't know. I'm not sure she can be much more help."

"Don't worry, we can take it from here," Garret said, feeling hopeful for the first time since he'd seen the blood on the street in front of Ashley's house. "I owe you."

When Garret and Doug had radioed to update the BOLO with a probable location and begun the two-plus-hour trip to Inks Lake, Garret glanced in the rearview mirror. The sight was a little overwhelming and pretty damned incredible. He'd expected the law enforcement officers who would help in the search. He'd expected the search and rescue dog and handler team. He'd even expected a few friends and family.

The caravan of vehicles that entered the highway went for what seemed like miles. There had to be twenty or more cars back there, each filled to capacity. It seemed the whole town of Evers had turned out. All for Ashley. And he got it. She was special. Beyond special. Despite her background, she'd opened her heart to others and had made all of these peoples' lives better for it. She brought something to their world they weren't willing to give up. And if that meant they needed to go search every inch of Inks Lake State Park, they would.

The drive was more time wasted, but at least he felt like he was moving toward her. Making progress of some kind. He only hoped it wasn't too late.

CHAPTER TWENTY-EIGHT

The call came as they approached the main road into the park. The state park rangers had located Michelle Davis's vehicle parked on one of the small access roads at the back of the park, just like Sheriff Davies predicted. They gave quick instructions for finding them and the entire entourage arrived minutes later. Garret was right behind Adam, the man handling Duke, the bloodhound they'd decided was the best first shot for trailing them into the woods. He kept pace with Adam as the dog kept its nose to the ground and plowed through the overgrown trail as fast as it could.

Garret didn't have to be a search and rescue handler to recognize the dog's body language. When Adam had given him a piece of Ashley's clothing to scent and the cue to seek, the dog had taken only seconds before his whole body went into action. He was clearly scenting and working toward a target, shoulders hunched as though he wanted to be closer to the ground. Closer to whatever it was his nose was taking in.

Adam held a long, bright orange line loosely in his hand and the two of them jogged to keep up with the dog. They had to slow eventually, when the overgrowth became too much to take at a fast clip, and Garret felt his frustration mounting once again.

How far in had the women gone? He began to wonder if maybe the dog was just wrong. Maybe the cabin was off the trail somewhere behind them and the dog had only kept going because the trail seemed to tell him to go that way. Although, when he thought about it, that was probably stupid. The dog had no concept of a trail as cut by humans in the woods. And John Davies had told him this dog and handler were the best of the best. Apparently, Adam Dean was some sort of legend, not only locally, but nationally.

It took all Garret had in him to trust the man and his dog. The trust paid off when the trail broke open to reveal a very small, broken-down cabin. Really, it was more of a shack, with busted windows and a roof that looked like it wouldn't hold out even the lightest of rain. Adam called the dog back to him and Garret was surprised to see the dog stop mid-trail and return to Adam. The man grinned when his dog put his paws up on his shoulders and took the treat he offered, followed by thorough ruffling of his sides and scruff. Garret didn't have time to wonder about the dog's manners.

He looked to the men who were coming up behind them quietly. They must have somehow convinced the entire cadre of Ashley's friends and families to wait until they knew what they were dealing with before following them up the trail. Doug, Sheriff Davies, and three of his deputies stood awaiting orders.

He signaled to indicate he and Doug would cover the front of the cabin, while the others should cover the sides and rear. Adam and Duke stayed behind on the trail as the men approached, and Garret had to work to still his breathing. He was used to the increased heart rate that came from approaching a dangerous situation, but in most cases he could easily regulate both and focus on the job at hand. Or at least he could ignore the heart rate and regulate the breathing such that it wasn't loud as a wind tunnel testing site.

Right now, he could hear the pounding of his blood coursing through his veins and every breath coming in what seemed like ragged gulps. His hand moved to the butt of his service weapon and he steadied himself as his thumb flicked open the safety catch of his holster. There were no signs of life from the cabin. No noise. No shadows or figures moving past the windows.

He moved to the side of the cabin, coming at an angle beside one of the windows as Doug covered him. He didn't need to look to know that the other officers would be taking up positions on the other side. He raised up and looked in the window, quickly scanning the single-room cabin. His heart stopped when he spotted the crumpled figure of a woman on the floor and the pool of blood beneath her. Long dark hair, slight build. He sucked in a breath as he scanned the remainder of the room. He heard the words of the other officers in his radio as they confirmed they saw no other people inside the structure. He felt a numbness he'd never known as they breached the cabin and he moved to check for a pulse.

His entire body felt as though it was dying, one piece at a time. His hands went numb, his feet, then heart. There was no pulse when he placed his fingers to her neck. He could see where one side of her neck had been gouged with a large piece of glass. Her body was cold. There would be no efforts to resuscitate, even as everything in him screamed to bring her back.

He felt the cups of coffee he'd been chugging all day toss in his stomach and he knew he'd be sick any minute. He was too late.

Too late to save her. Too late to tell her how he felt about her. Too late to tell her he wanted so much more with her. He was about to turn away from her, not wanting to have the image of Ashley's dead body etched forever in his brain, when his brain clicked back into gear and began to process what he was seeing.

The hair was dark, but it was shorter and stringy, not glossy and full. The body was a little too tall and heavier set than Ashley was. He reach out and flipped the body. It was Michelle Davis. The dead woman was Michelle Davis, not his Ashley.

His eyes met Doug's, who stood above him.

"It's not Ashley!" Doug called out to the others. Garret

knew they were all thinking the same thing. If Michelle was dead, who had Ashley?

Garret swore as he stalked from the cabin. Adam was jogging up to the front of the cabin, Duke in tow. He must have been radioed by one of the men inside. Garret clenched his jaw as he watched Adam pull the sealed bag that contained a swatch of Ashley's clothing from his vest. He let the dog scent the article again and then gave the signal to search. And, once again, Garret followed, keeping pace with handler and dog, praying the dog could work his magic one more time.

CHAPTER TWENTY-NINE

This time, as soon as they hit the woods, they had to slow to a crawl. Or, what felt like a crawl. Though the trail they'd followed coming up had been narrow, at least it was a trail. Here, there was nothing. The brush was knee high and thick. But Garret could see where someone else had crashed through here earlier. The damage made it apparent. He wished he knew enough about tracking to be able to tell if it was one person or two, or a large person or small. Hell, he didn't even know enough to know if deciphering those details was possible. He wanted to know if Ashley had left on her own or was taken by someone. Bill Franks might still be in prison, but he didn't know if Michelle Davis had someone else working with her or not.

He didn't know why Ashley had gone this way instead of back down the trail, unless she was being followed. The thought of her being pursued rekindled his fear and stoked it to a roaring inferno. It was not at all the way he was used to feeling. Even when they'd had a missing child case a few years back, he'd been able to handle it with nerves of steel and a calm perseverance that brought the child home safely.

Right now, he'd give anything to find that detached calm as Doug and he followed Adam and the dog over logs and brush. By now, he could hear the group of additional searchers being assembled behind them. He knew from experience, they'd be assigned a section of a grid, each walking only feet from one another, looking for signs of Ashley. They would do as he, Adam, and Doug were doing now, calling Ashley's name every minute, hoping—straining —to hear some sound. Any sound. Anything to lead them to her.

ASHLEY TRIED to focus on putting one foot in front of the other, but each movement brought a throbbing pain from one of her injuries. Whether it was her head, her hand, or her ankle, something was constantly shooting a painful reminder to her that she needed to find help. Quickly.

But nothing was happening quickly right now. Picking her way through the thick underbrush was slow going. This wasn't a casual walk in the woods. The brush came to just above her knee and the sad excuses for shoes she had on were providing very little protection from the branches and roots stabbing at her feet and ankles.

She had forgotten about her hunger a while back, but thirst still plagued her and she was fending off dizziness.

She'd spent a little time trying to find the path they'd taken to get to the cabin, thinking if she hiked in what she thought was an easterly direction, she should hit it. She not only didn't hit it, she became more disoriented the more she tried to find her way. When she'd given up on finding the trail, she'd gone back to heading toward what she thought was south, but she hadn't hit the road at all. In fact, she was fairly sure she might have gone in a big circle at one point.

Ashley could see the trees begin to thin up ahead and she hoped that meant she was coming to a populated area where she might find people hiking. Or if she was in a state park as she suspected, she might find people swimming at one of the lakes in the region. It would make sense for the trees to thin out as she neared either a lake or a river or something. Wouldn't it?

The dizziness was beginning to be coupled with nausea and her muscles were cramping. She kept her eyes on the spot she could see ahead, where the sky opened up more. She couldn't hear any signs of activity, but she didn't let that deter her as she kept moving forward. What she wouldn't give to be in Garret's arms right now. To know he was here to care for her, to keep her safe. She felt so safe in his arms.

She needed that right now. She needed to feel protected again. Ashley shook her head, as she began to slow her pace. She felt confused and she raised her hand to her head wound, trying to feel if the bleeding had started up again. She winced at the contact, light as it was. She stopped for a minute, just for a minute to catch her breath.

"No," she said out loud to the trees around her. She

began moving again. Moving seemed important now. It seemed crucial that she just keep moving.

She began to laugh then because all she could hear was Dory, the blue fish from Nemo, singing *just keep swimming, just keep swimming* over and over in her head. Garret would see the humor in that.

"Wait." She was talking to herself again. "That's the wrong way." She wasn't facing the area where the trees opened up any longer. She'd gotten turned around somehow. She turned to see if she could find the right direction. *Just keep swimming, just keep swimming.* So funny.

She turned again, hoping to find the right direction to go. She had to keep moving. Turned again. And then the world started spinning faster than she could handle and Ashley hunched over, throwing one arm out toward a tree to try to catch onto something. If she could just find something solid to hold onto, she'd be okay. But the tree wasn't there. Her fingers seemed to grasp at air and her stomach spun as she went down.

CHAPTER THIRTY

Cora looked around at the group of people gathered in the woods, waiting for news of Ashley. They weren't allowed to help with the search. Not as long as there might still be a criminal out there. They wouldn't be allowed in the woods to search unless the police decided there was no longer a threat, but they were all gathered. Waiting.

Her parents, sister, and brothers. Justin Kensington and several of his friends flanked her on the other side. She couldn't believe this was happening. The whole thing felt like a bad dream, only she didn't seem to be able to wake up.

"Hey, Cora," Justin said from beside her. "We'll find her. She'll be all right."

She just nodded and wiped her nose with her sleeve like a child.

"Come here," he said and pulled her into a hug. She

shoved away from him. She didn't want his sympathy right now. She didn't want anything other than to find her sister.

"I'm fine," she said, ignoring the startled look on Justin's face. She didn't care if he was shocked she would pull away from him. He probably expected her to fall all over him like she usually did, but she didn't want to do that right now. She didn't care about her stupid crush on Justin or the way she always wished he'd treat her as more than a friend. She just wanted to find Ashley and bring her home safely.

She walked back toward her car, not wanting to be near the others any longer. She should have noticed something was wrong. For a whole day, she hadn't noticed something was wrong. Nor said anything to anyone, even though she'd known right away that Ashley was lying to her in her texts. They theorized now that it had been Michelle Davis texting everyone with Ashley's phone, so that no one would realize Ashley had been taken.

But Cora should have known. She should have recognized it wasn't Ashley. She'd even known the text was a lie, and yet she'd still believed Ashley had written it. She hadn't called her sister on the lie. She hadn't even thought to suspect it might not be Ashley. She'd done nothing. And because of it, Ashley could now be hurt, dead, or in the hands of anyone. For all they knew, Michelle Davis had had some crackhead helping her and he'd taken an interest in Ashley. Maybe he'd killed Michelle and dragged Ashley into the woods and he was—

Justin caught her hand as she walked away, pulling her up by his side as they started toward the sound of shouts coming from one of the patrol car radios. The search dog was barking and Cora hoped that meant he'd found something. Justin squeezed her hand as they all stared at the source of the sound, waiting, wishing for some indication that Ashley was alive and safe. For some news.

GARRET MADE it to Ashley first, scanning the pale skin and drenched clothing. She was wet with perspiration and her heart rate felt more like a bird's than a person's. She was in rough shape. He spotted several injuries right off the bat, but what concerned him most were the obvious signs of heat exhaustion. If left untreated, it could move to heat stroke. And he would guess she had no water in her system. One hand was wrapped in a blood-soaked shirt.

Her eyes were open and she looked at him, but she seemed dazed and disoriented. He heard her say something about swimming, but then her eyes closed.

He heard the radio call for an ambulance behind him. Adam was next to him, unwrapping her hand, then expertly packing gauze and wrapping the large gash on her palm as Garret tried to get her to wake up and talk to him.

"Ashley, come on back to us, hon. Open up your eyes and talk to me again." He could hear the way his voice was shaking. Shit, he was so far off his game, he didn't know if he'd ever get his edge back, but he didn't care. He just wanted Ashley back.

Her eyes fluttered and she opened them, looking

around, and this time she seemed to be gripped with panic, in wild-eyed confusion. He put his hands on her shoulders and gently pinned her in place. "Don't get up yet. You're safe. We've got an ambulance on the way."

And then, as a path was cleared and a backboard brought up for her, he continued to talk to her, telling her everything they'd do when they got her out of there. She watched him the whole time, but he wasn't sure she heard him. Adam started fluids and checked vitals, seemingly a machine at this, able to function despite their surroundings.

Twelve men took turns carrying her off the hill. It turned out the area she'd been lost in was no more than a few miles from the road. She'd simply been so disoriented, she hadn't found her way to the populated parts of the park. Adam seemed matter-of-fact when he told Garret it happened all the time. But Garret didn't feel matter-of-fact about any of this. All he could think on the ambulance ride to the hospital was how close he'd come to losing this woman. The woman who now seemed to be such a part of his life, he didn't know how he'd ever let her go if she didn't want the same thing he did. A life together. A future together. Family and home and hearth and all that sappy damned stuff neither of them had had for much of their lives. He wanted it all.

CHAPTER THIRTY-ONE

The first time Ashley woke up in the hospital, Garret felt a rage he'd never known before. And sadly, the woman it was directed toward was dead. There was no one he could take his wrath out on. Ashley woke up terrified, crying out, and he could picture how lost and frightened she'd been in those woods. It was as if she was living it all over again in front of him. He watched helplessly as her mother brushed away her tears and kissed her head and shushed Ashley back to sleep.

Just before she shut her eyes, she met his gaze and he tried to quell the anger so she wouldn't see it. He watched her eyes flutter closed, then took up his vigil in a chair in the corner. She slept for hours and he worked on clearing his mind. Trying not to think of the injustice of what she'd been through. After surviving her childhood, it just didn't seem right that she had to go through this now. That she had one more thing to survive. One more thing to haunt her.

When she woke again, she asked for him instead of crying out and his heart kicked over in his chest.

"Where is Garret?" Her voice was scratchy despite the water her mom had given her.

He stood and stepped closer. "I'm here, Ash." He moved to take Cora's place next to Ashley and took her hand in his.

"I look so bad that you have to stay all the way over there?" Her smile was wide and she looked beautiful to him, despite the stitches and the way her hair had been shaved on one side.

"Never," he said and ran a finger down the less bruised side of her face. "You're gorgeous."

"Okay, but I want you to know I'm gonna milk this for all it's worth. I want breakfast in bed, and cookies and ice cream. Oh, and chocolate. Lots of chocolate."

Garret grinned at her. She was back. She wasn't going to let this keep her down. God, he loved this woman. Loved her. Heart and soul, body, mind, all that crap. Loved the hell out of her. "I'll call Johnny Depp and have him get right on all of that."

Her laugh was real and genuine and deep, just the way he hoped it would be.

And so he took a gamble. The gamble of a lifetime. "How about diamonds? Can we throw diamonds on that list? Maybe in the form of a ring?"

Her eyes went big and round and he held his breath. And then she faked a scowl. "Really? That's the best you can do? You get that I write romance novels for a living, right? I need more than, 'hey, you want a diamond with your ice cream?' You get that, right?"

Cora piped up behind him. "I can help him. We'll work on flowers, wine, the ring, the whole nine yards."

"Maybe a few candles," her mom added.

Garret nodded. "I can do candles."

"Let me know when you get it together, and I'll think about it." Ashley's cheeky response was all he needed to know she'd be okay. She was going to get past this. She was going to be his.

EPILOGUE

Ashley laughed as Garret swung her in a circle. What they were doing couldn't really be called dancing. They were abysmally bad at it, but they had fun and she was in his arms, and that's really all that mattered. He dipped her at the end of the song and placed an exaggerated smacking kiss to her lips. This was her hero. Her romance novel happy ending. And she wouldn't have him any other way.

"Come on," he said as he pulled her from the makeshift dance floor Cade and Shane Bishop had set up at the Bishop ranch. It was Laura Bishop's birthday and it seemed like the whole town had come out for the barbeque. "Let's get you more of that cake."

A man after her own heart, she thought as he tugged her over to the dessert table again. This was their second trip through. But let's face it, who could resist apple pie and cake?

"Hey, Ashley, Garret," said John Davies, approaching the two with a nod as they walked with laden plates to one of the picnic tables. "Got a minute, Garret?"

"Sure," Garret said with a smile. "Sit with us?"

"You bet."

Ashley dug into the chocolate cake she'd taken just a sliver of as she waited to hear what John had to say.

"I wanted to let you know Evers is going to be funding its own police force soon. The population has grown to the point where it no longer makes sense to have the sheriff's office as a satellite here. The town needs its own force. Its own chief of police and probably two to three deputies."

"That's great, John. Are you planning to throw your hat in there for chief?" Garret asked. Garret was on leave from the Branson Falls department. When his captain had discovered his relationship with Alice and it had come out that he also was having a relationship with Ashley, he'd been suspended without pay, pending a hearing. Garret had just been happy he'd been able to cover for Doug and convince his superiors Doug hadn't known about any of it.

"No, but I'm hoping you will. Actually, the whole town council is hoping you will. Your name is at the top of our list. Is it something you'd consider?"

Garret looked at Ashley and she wondered if he would want that. Small-town police chief instead of detective in a larger city? What she really wondered was whether he'd want to be near her, close by so they could spend more time together with a lot less travel. Maybe live together. She found herself holding her breath as she waited for his answer.

"You realize I was suspended for weeks, right? I mean, you guys get that? I might be back at work, but I'm not exactly the most highly recommended officer in the state right now."

"We know." John nodded. "Your record prior to this case speaks for itself. We want you."

"Can I let you know in a few days?" Garret asked John, and Ashley felt her stomach drop. Maybe he didn't want to be closer to her. Or maybe he did but he didn't want to move here. Maybe he wanted her to move to Branson Falls with him.

Her writing career was portable, but she loved her job at the library and her whole family was here. Would she be able to move? To be happy in Branson Falls? Garret squeezed her hand and she realized John had said his good-byes and walked away.

"You all right, hon?" Garret asked, and as she looked at him, she knew she'd move anywhere for him. She'd hate it. But she'd do it if it meant being with him. He was her happily ever after. He was her everything.

She nodded and took a bite of the apple pie that was squished onto her plate alongside the cake and cookies. "I'm great." And she was.

She'd left behind the fear that had plagued her after the kidnapping. She had been back to see her counselor and had talked through what she was feeling instead of bottling it up. She'd taken some anti-anxiety medication at first, but after two months, the tricks her counselor had taught her for calming herself had been enough to wean off the meds. And it didn't hurt that Garret was with her whenever he could be. By her side, making her feel safe and secure.

The caseworkers had located extended family for Evie Davis—a cousin of her mother's—who was not only willing to take her in, but happy to have her. She'd relocated to Vermont to live with the cousin. They weren't legally able to get updates from social services, but Garret had gotten an update from a friend on the sly. Evie was doing well, and that's all Ashley could hope for.

Bill Franks was still in prison. The state had decided to try him for aggravated manslaughter for the death of her baby. She would need to testify eventually, but for now, she decided against thinking about him. He wasn't worth it.

Garret leaned in and kissed the spot behind her ear that made her eyes cross and her breath come in pants. She turned her head into his chest to muffle the moan that slipped from her lips. She could never hide her response from him, but she thought maybe it was a good idea to hide it from the rest of the party-goers.

"Ready to head home?" His question came in the gravel-roughened tone that told her what he had in mind for when they arrived there, and she nodded against his chest.

"Let me get rid of these," he said, taking their plates and walking to one of the garbage bags hanging from a stick wedged in the ground. She didn't even care that he'd taken her desserts from her. Not when she knew what he had planned for her at home.

GARRET STUCK his key in the front door of Ashley's house and tugged her inside behind him. The outside light had come on when they pulled in the drive and he'd left the hallway light on, but other than that, the house was dark. He pressed her against the closed door, kissing her long and deep. She responded just as he liked, with her whole body. She melted into him, pressing all those curves into just the right places. He ground his hips into her. He needed to get her to the bedroom, but she'd been teasing him the whole way home, her hands tormenting his tortured erection through his pants as he drove.

It was a miracle he hadn't driven off the road. Those sinful hands threaded through his hair and she pulled slightly, drawing a growl from him. But it was the best kind of growl. The one that said he'd be taking her on the couch or the floor, because making it to her bedroom wasn't an option.

And then she bit his lower lip, and it was over. He stripped her down and undid the belt and fly of his pants. He should probably be ashamed that he didn't get his pants all the way off, but as he buried his head in her chest, devouring her nipples one at a time, his cock found her wet heat and sank into her. He didn't know when he had lifted her and he hadn't realized she'd wrapped her legs around his waist until he found himself buried within her, her back pressed against the door.

She nipped his ear with that wayward mouth of hers

that never wanted to behave and he was lost, plunging again and again. Her direction—harder, deeper, more—drove him into her and when she shouted his name and her muscles clenched around him, he was done. He came hard, holding himself deep within her body as the waves washed through him.

"Christ, Ashley. What you do to me."

She laughed. Laughed as if reveling in the power she had over him. He only hoped she didn't crush his heart with that power. He pulled back and kissed her, gently this time. Soft and long while they were still connected together in the most intimate of ways.

"I was supposed to get you to the bedroom."

"Why is that?" she asked. "I like the wall." She wiggled her hips on him as she said it and he felt himself begin to come to life again. He didn't know how that was possible, but hell if he'd complain.

Focus. "I have a surprise in the bedroom." He groaned when she licked at his neck.

"I thought you just gave me my surprise," she whispered, the vixen fully engaged tonight. God, he loved her when she was like this. Hell, he loved her any way she wanted to be.

He lifted her off of him, ignoring the pout she gave him, and pulled his shirt over his head. He placed it on her, then kissed her. "Wait right here. I'll be right back."

He shucked his pants and boxers since their current position around his thighs wasn't conducive to walking, and headed for the bedroom. He had prepped everything ahead of time before picking her up at the library that afternoon. It took only minutes to light the candles and return to her.

"What are you up to, Garret Hensley?" she asked, her full-blown librarian voice on board. Why that shot straight to his cock, he would never know. He pulled her down the hall to the bedroom.

When they stepped into the room, she gasped, and he knew she was taking in the candles, the rose petals on the bed, the jewelers' box sitting on her pillow. He went to the edge of the bed and sat, pulling her into his arms. He reached beside him for the box and opened it to show her the solitaire diamond ring set in platinum.

When he looked at her face, there were tears shimmering in her eyes. "I hope those are happy tears," he said.

She didn't speak, but nodded vigorously, and he laughed, then slipped the ring from the box and put it on her finger.

"You've made me the happiest man in the world simply by letting me be in your life. But if you say yes to making it official, to making this permanent and building a family with me, you'll make me even happier. Marry me, Ashley Walker?"

She nodded again and he couldn't help the laugh that came from deep within him. He meant what he said. He'd never been happier. And it was all her doing.

"I love you, Ashley."

"I love you, Garret," she finally said, wrapping her arms around his neck and nuzzling her face to his. His body had already been primed and ready for her, but her simple act brought out the raging primal need to be inside of her again. His vixen had other things in mind. She lifted herself and took hold of him, slipping his hard length between her legs so he jutted up along her wet slit. She began to move her hips in small circles, teasing and taunting him with a gleam in her eyes.

"If you loved me, you wouldn't torment me like that."

All he got in answer was a soft moan as she continued, adding her hand, her palm skimming the head of his cock as she moved.

"Evil, demon woman." He said the words, but they weren't harsh. And he felt nothing but love for her as he slipped his shirt off her. He grasped her by the waist and tossed her on the bed, then moved over her to begin some torture of his own.

He spent some leisurely time working his way with his lips and tongue down her neck, her shoulder, the slope of one breast, then the other. When he bit down lightly on one nipple, grazing the tight bud with his teeth, she pushed up into him with her hips on a groan. He laughed. He planned to thoroughly enjoy this and wasn't about to let her rush him.

He quickly realized he'd have to pin her hands if he wanted to have his way with her, but he didn't mind. He grasped her wrists together, having a somewhat caveman-like reaction to the flash of his ring on her finger, before raising her hands above her head and holding them there. He continued to worship her breasts, loving the perfect round globes and the pink nipples that seemed to strain for more attention from him.

He wanted nothing more than to love on her like this forever, but there were other parts of her body calling to him. He released her hands as he worked his way down, kissing a trail as he went. He stopped and pressed his face into the softest part of her stomach, something that always made her squirm, but it was one of his favorite things to do. He loved the soft feel of her. Loved how her body felt so welcoming to his.

"Stop," she said with a giggle and pushed his head away. Always the response he got, and he loved that, too. He nipped her skin in punishment and continued down her torso, spreading her legs wide. He stopped to look at the gorgeous folds and the hooded tangle of nerves waiting for him. She was so damned gorgeous, she took his breath away. He licked her from the base of her slit to her clitoris, then circled and suckled as she writhed beneath him.

One finger, then two, slipped inside of her as he clamped down and suckled hard, and she burst for him, just as he'd hoped she would. Her body flew beneath him as her hips moved with the orgasm. He marveled at the look on her face, then kissed her mouth while she came back down to earth. He raised himself above her, looping one knee up over his arm and sheathing himself inside of her.

"I love you, Garret," she said as she laced her arms around his neck and pulled him close. He kept his pace slow, leisurely withdrawing from her, before slowly—so damned slowly, he thought it might kill him—pushing back into her.

"I love you, too," he said, his eyes locked to hers as they began to move as one. Within minutes, they were both sent flying over the edge, this time, going together.

When they caught their breath and Garret had Ashley tucked into the curve of his body, his chest to her back, her backside snug against his hips, she sighed. It was the kind of sigh he loved to hear from her. The one that told him she was deeply satisfied. Content and happy, and he loved to know he'd put her in that state. And now he'd get to spend the rest of his life doing that, bringing her happiness.

"What do you think of me throwing my name in the ring for chief and relocating here permanently?"

She twisted in his arms and turned those gorgeous blue eyes on him. "You'd do that? Would you be happy with the job? The small town? The slower pace?"

"Yes, yes, and yes," he said, laughter sneaking its way into his voice. "I'd love the job. New challenges and the chance to build my own team. I might just see if Doug is interested. I love the town, and as for the pace, I'm not sure it will be slower. Just different. But either way, slow is good, Ash. I need more time to spend with you. Time to start a family. Time to build our life together. And we need to be near your family."

"We do?" she asked, eyes round as though she couldn't believe he would take her family and her roots in this town into consideration.

"Of course we do. You need them, and they need you.

Hell, this town needs you. Where else would they find a hell-raising, soft-porn-writing, kick-ass librarian?"

She smacked his chest. "I do not write soft porn!"

He grinned and wiggled his eyebrows. "Yes, you do. I've read it." He dropped a kiss to her lips. "I loved it. I hope to inspire more of it. I'm at your disposal day or night for research and testing anytime."

She harrumphed at him and he laughed, pulling her close.

"So, yes to the chief thing? Yes to relocating?"

She looked into his eyes and nodded. "Yes to it all, Garret Hensley. Yes to it all."

Dear Reader,

Fun fact about writing: some stories come to you as if the characters told you it themselves. Ashley told me her story on a walk one day and it was such a powerful one, I knew I had to write it, even though it was a hard topic to write. Thank you for reading it.

Next up in the series is a novella with Carter, one of the sheriff's deputies. He and his heroine, Lily, are going to have to work fast to take down an illegal dog racing ring. You can get Honor and Protect here! loriryanromance.com/book/Honor-and-Protect

Read on for chapter one of Honor and Protect:

CHAPTER ONE

Lily Winn didn't doubt herself very often, but right about now seemed like a damned good time to start. She'd seen plenty of birds flap their wings in a blind panic against the bars of a cage, their fear palpable and real. She was sure if she could crack open her chest and peek at her heart, that's what it would look like right now. Clattering against the bars of her ribcage trying to make a run for it. When her friend had called and told her she suspected there might be illegal dog racing happening in the area, Lily's bright idea to go poking around abandoned farms or ranchland in the area surrounding Evers, Texas had seemed brilliant.

She gripped the empty dog collar and leash she carried in her fist as a cover story and glanced around the property, debating just how stupid it was to step out into the clearing. Probably very. When she'd parked her Jeep out on the road and hiked in, she'd figured anyone stopping her would buy the story about looking for a lost dog. She was dressed for a hike, with khaki shorts, hiking boots, and her honey-blonde hair pulled back in a braid. She knew people saw her as the typical "girl next door" and she hoped that innocent look would play to her advantage here. The collar and leash were well-worn from use around her clinic. She thought the story would make a convincing one.

Now she wondered if anyone she ran into might shoot first and ask questions later. She hadn't lived in Texas very long, but her impression was that many of the natives around here might not spend a whole lot of time chatting up a stranger on their land. They'd shoot first and fast and without a lick of warning.

If she hadn't heard the whimpering just then, she might have remained frozen long enough to convince herself to turn back. If there was one thing Lily knew, it was the sound of an animal in pain. And it was the one thing she could never turn her back on—an animal in pain. Any animal.

With one final glance around, she stepped out of the woods and into the clearing that surrounded the old barn and its rundown corrals. The place looked abandoned, just as she'd been told. She hoped so. Because she didn't think she'd be able to carry off the lie about looking for her dog at this point. Not while her voice was shaking. Heck, her whole body was shaking.

Stupid, stupid, stupid, she chanted in her head as she pictured all of the horror movies with heroines who went into the dark room after hearing a noise no matter how much Lily yelled at the screen. No matter how stupid and foolish she told them they were, those horror movie chicks stepped forward into certain danger. As she was doing right now. *Great.* She was the stupid girl in the horror movie doing what everyone with half a brain knew you shouldn't.

Each breath sounded in her ears, jagged and raw, as she crossed the open space between corrals, moving toward the barn. Toward the source of the dog's cries. Closer and closer. Praying the barn was empty. Praying no one would pop out any minute. Or worse, simply shoot from where they stood. No, surely they would warn her first. Right?

She stopped in her tracks, listening to the sounds around her, blocking out the rasp of her own labored breathing. It wasn't the hike in that had done this to her. Even though it had been a half mile or more, she was fit. She'd taken it at a good clip. But this was fear, plain and simple. Maybe the bad guys wouldn't hear her gulps of air? Maybe it was only in her head.

The dog's cries came from around the side of the barn, drawing Lily's focus back to her goal. She edged toward the whimpering, creeping closer to the corner of the barn. If there was someone around that corner, she hadn't a clue how she'd handle that. She had no weapon. Nothing but her empty dog collar and leash and her cell phone shoved in her back pocket. The smart girl—the one who was still alive at the end of the horror movie—probably would have called for help. She'd have backed away and gone out to the car to wait for someone else to arrive.

But who would Lily call? She didn't have many friends in town. She'd relocated to Evers to take over her grandfather's veterinary practice when he retired. He was housebound now after suffering a stroke. With her efforts to bring the practice up to date, she hadn't so much as poked her head out of the office.

She'd only met Mary Greene, who had warned her about the dog racing, because Mary brought rescue dogs into the clinic for discounted shots and spay and neuter. They chatted in the clinic but hadn't gotten together yet outside of it. She suspected Mary devoted most of her time to her full-time job and her rescue efforts. She likely didn't socialize all that much either.

It's not like Lily could call the police and tell them she needed help for a whimpering dog. They'd laugh at her. So, heart still pounding against the bars of its cage, she eased around the corner of the barn.

Nothing.

Not a person in sight, but also no sign of a dog. She could hear it more clearly now, and it must have smelled her presence because it began to yip loudly. A high-pitched, plaintive yip. She stepped out from the relative protection of the barn, such as it was, and scanned the area.

There. Lily didn't give thought to her safety as she rushed to the edge of a large ditch that looked like it had been dug by man, and not through any occurrence of nature.

"Oh no, no, no, no, no, no." She slipped and slid down the bank and wanted to close her eyes. Wanted to erase the sight before her. At least four other dogs lay in the ditch, but they were so clearly beyond her help, she didn't stop to check on them. She gritted her teeth as she ignored the flies that didn't seem the least bit bothered by her invasion, and made her way to the dog whose eyes were trained on her. There was pain in those eyes, but also hope. Lily quickly took in the injured back leg. It had been shot, the wound festering and necrotic. The leg was hanging, unusable. She knew without further inspection she'd need to remove it.

"This is going to hurt a little, baby girl, but I'll get you something to help with that soon."

Lily's hands worked quickly as she used her leash to make a makeshift muzzle for the dog. She didn't seem aggressive so far, but when Lily went to move her there'd be a lot of pain. A dog in pain can always bite. That was a lesson Lily had learned early and learned well. If she ever forgot it, she had the faint scars of a bite on her left wrist to remind her. The cream-colored dog had the markings of Saluki and Greyhound in her genes, with long, darker hair on her ears and tail, and a short coat covering her body. She had a thicker body than those breeds, though, so she might also have some Lab or something else in her. It was common practice in the world of underground dog racing to breed Greyhounds with other dog breeds to take advantage of the speed of the Greyhound's build, while making the mix sturdier to withstand the rigors of racing in empty fields. The dogs were called longdogs or lurchers, depending on the mix.

Lily used the thin button-up shirt she always wore over a tee at the office to tightly bind the leg. "Aren't you sweet, honey girl? Maybe that's what we'll call you," she crooned as the dog held remarkably still while Lily worked on her. "Honey," she said.

She stood and looked at the ground rising up in front of her. She would need to climb out of the ditch first, then try to drag the dog up the side. "I'm so sorry," she murmured, then stuck one foot into a divot in the mud wall in front of her and hoisted herself up and over the edge. The next part would suck for the dog. Royally suck. Lily laid on her stomach, shimmying forward as far as she could without falling into the hole again, and reached down toward Honey. She grasped her front legs, all the while keeping her focus on the soft trusting eyes of the incredible creature. She had to focus on that. If she focused on anything else, she'd see the dead eyes of the other animals in the pit. They had likely been tossed in here and shot. Honey was the only one who had held on long enough for Lily to have a shot at saving her.

She stumbled under the weight of the dog when she first lifted her, but once hoisted in her arms, it wasn't so bad. Lily was strong and used to moving animals whose full weight hung limp under sedation. Sure, she typically had help, and didn't have to walk half a mile, but she wasn't about to leave Honey here and risk whoever had shot those dogs coming back to finish her off. Walking as quickly as she could, Lily cut back through the woods and out to the road. She needed to get Honey back to her clinic. She'd lose the leg, for sure. If Lily got lucky, though, maybe it wasn't too late to save Honey's life.

GET HONOR AND PROTECT HERE!

loriryanromance.com/book/Honor-and-Protect

IF YOU'VE ALREADY READ Honor and Protect or you want to skip the novella, you're ready for Desire and Protect. Cade's brother, Shane Bishop, gets his turn in this novel. I know you've been waiting to see what happened to him. Well, let me just say, that buttoned-up lawyer met his match. <u>Grab Desire and Protect here!</u> loriryanromance.-com/book/Desire-and-Protect

As ALWAYS, thank you to my husband and children for putting up with me. It's really not easy.

Thank you Kate and Melanie for your invaluable input during the drafting and beta phases, and to Kate for correcting my search and rescue errors. I'm pretty sure I changed everything you said to change!

Thank you Dr. Ashley B. Hampton for making sure I didn't get the mental health stuff all mucked up! It seems I'm always needing your advice these days. Note to self: write characters who don't require a psychologist every once in a while. ;)

Thank you to Beverly Stradley for her geography help. By the way, there is no private land with a cabin at the back of Inks Lake. I made that up!

Thank you to John Bartholomew once again for his medical expertise and answering my questions on the fly.

When I first began this project over two years ago, there was a lovely lady on Facebook who answered my questions about social work and some of the regulations and require-ments that would apply to this story. I can't for the life of me find her name! I hate not being able to thank her personally, but if that was you, I'm very grateful for the help. The fact that perfect strangers will answer my calls for help means the world.

ABOUT THE AUTHOR

Lori Ryan is a NY Times and USA Today bestselling author who writes romantic suspense, contemporary romance, and sports romance. She lives with an extremely understanding husband, three wonderful children, and two mostly-behaved dogs in Austin, Texas. It's a bit of a zoo, but she wouldn't change a thing.

Lori published her first novel in April of 2013 and hasn't looked back since then. She loves to connect with her readers.

For new release info and bonus content, join her newsletter here: loriryanromance.com/lets-keep-touch.

Follow her online:

facebook.com/loriryanromance
twitter.com/Loriryanauthor
instagram.com/loriryanauthor